ELEPHANT @ THE PARTY

ELEPHANT@
THE PARTY

JULIE D'AMOUR

Copyright © Julie D'Amour 2015

The moral right of Julie D'Amour to be identified as the author has been asserted in accordance with the Copyright, Designs and Patents Act 1988.

This book is entirely a work of fiction. The names, characters and incidents portrayed in it are the work of the author's imagination. Any resemblance to actual persons, living or dead, events or localities are entirely coincidental.

Set in Baskerville

Designed and typeset by
Couper Street Type Co.

For Matthew and Sarah,
angels that light up my life.

CHAPTER ONE

So this is it my first kiss. It's not at all how I imagined. It's not in a crimson-walled Arabian tent with low plinths layered in the finest jewel-colored silks and velvets, adorned with a million pillows scattered all around in emerald, sapphire and amethyst. Nor I am lounging in a little gauzy number, something that brings out the color of my eyes, makes my skin glow and miraculously makes all signs of excess cake eating and face stuffing disappear, whilst Jonny Simpson prowls towards me with panther-like grace, wearing nothing but black silk drawstring trousers and a jewel-encrusted sword, bending to taste my lips which he says are "sweeter than honey and more delicious than the plumpest date".

Nor am I standing at the top of a windswept moor, where Jonny is striding determinedly towards me through the purple heather, dressed in riding boots, calf-skin breeches and a lawn shirt with expertly tied cravat. He must be in a hurry, for a gentleman does not go without waistcoat and over-jacket or perhaps, I muse with glee, he is no gentleman after all. He is marching up the hill to promise undying love to me. "I can wait no longer Lucy, I must kiss you now," he declares as he bends me backwards and kisses me ravenously.

Nor have I been kidnapped by the Lord of the Underworld, dragged to his infernal palace and tied to a wooden post. My skin shimmers enticingly as if oiled as sweat pours down my body. My white chiffon dress is ripped, but modestly covering all the important bits. The Dark Lord stands over me demanding I surrender to him, but I will die first. As the last of my life force ebbs away I become vaguely aware of a battle raging around me, the ring of steel against steel. Then silence as a pair of magnificent silver-tipped wings shields me from the heat. I am flying higher and higher; gone is the burning fetid air, only the bluest sky and intoxicating freshness. The strong sculpted arms of my avenging angel surround me. "Jonny," I whisper against his rock-hard chest.

His feet land softly on the earth. "Lucy, if anything were to happen to you...I couldn't bear it," he declares, meshing his lips hungrily with mine.

I am about five minutes away from turning sixteen, about five feet away from my first kiss, and the pair of lips heading my way belong not to my ultimate fantasy but to his brother.

I am standing under an ancient weeping willow at the very bottom of my garden. The tree is prettily lit by fairy lights strung from its branches and wind chimes sing softly in the icy breeze. A few eager flakes herald the arrival of snow, and my breath escapes in great fluffy clouds.

Gregor steps towards me. He pulls me gently against his body as one hand dangles a sprig of mistletoe above our heads. My brain is whirring and spinning, a billion wondrous thoughts running amok. All of which stop as Gregor's lips tenderly touch mine. He moves away a fraction as I draw in a surprised breath. Changing angle, our lips meet again.

Nothing else exists at this moment in time and space. Nothing but the unexpected jolt of electricity sparking through my body. Nothing but the slowly increasing pressure of Gregor's lips against mine. Nothing but my body's need to close the non-existent gap between us.

I notice nothing else when Gregor swipes his tongue against my lower lip and my mouth opens, like a flower gently unfolding with the morning sun. My arms snake around Gregor's neck, hands sliding to tease the silky ends of his hair. My body arches against his as his tongue gently probes and flicks over mine. My breasts tingle, my thighs tighten and press together as our dancing tongues move from a shy waltz to a furious tango.

Simultaneously we pull apart, gasping like landed fish. As he straightens, a huge grin spreads across his face.

"Not bad, eh?"

"It was alright," I concede.

"Alright?" His voice goes up an octave or five. "You've got to be joking, Luce. That was the best kiss I've ever had."

"OK, I'll admit it was pretty great. Not that I've anything to compare it to."

"I guess great is OK, but I was aiming for totally freaking awesome. I obviously need more practice. Want to try again?"

With unusual cool, I keep him dangling. I scuff my foot through the dead leaves and gaze at him through lowered lashes.

"OK."

We move back together and embrace for another spine melting, mind-numbing, world-spinning or possibly ending, kiss. My life as I know it has certainly just ended.

"Hurry up you two, it's nearly midnight." We spring apart as Gregor's mum calls to us from the kitchen door. "You can get down to more snogging after the bells."

"Oh my God, has she been watching us?" I cover my reddening face then peek through my fingers.

"Looks like she's not the only one."

I turn towards the kitchen window. My mum and Gregor's are both grinning manically, raising their champagne glasses at us in a silent toast.

Gregor takes my hand and gently tugs. "Come on, I'll protect you."

The kiss must have knocked me for six. My legs are shaking so badly I think they might buckle. Sweat is breaking out across my forehead. I'm hot and dizzy, really dizzy.

"Lucy, are you OK?" Gregor tries to grab my elbow but it's not there anymore. My bones have gone, disintegrated, *poof*. There's nothing left to hold my body up. I am crumpling, falling into a black hole. I reach the bottom with a thump, *oowff*.

CHAPTER TWO

An awful groaning noise escapes my lips. "Oh god, my head," I moan, attempting to move my stiff cold body off the damp earth. Every inch of me aches, and I'm hungry. I'd better get up or there won't be any food left at the buffet. I crank my sticky eyes open and wince as light blinds me. I will myself to roll onto my side and sit up, shielding my eyes with my hand as I take in the verdant scenery and soft afternoon sunlight.

"Hell-oh," calls a soft lilting voice.

I screw up my eyes, turn my head towards the owner and let out a terrified scream.

"Who are you?" I demand, staring at the thing before me.

Sitting on a boulder next me is a creature unlike anything I've ever seen. He has the most incredible and defined bone structure. His skin is silver and luminescent as if someone has skimmed the surface of the moon and molded a man. His hair is an impossible golden-silver. His body is tall, lean and angular. His ears are elongated and pointed at the top. His eyes are teal, a magnificent blue-green, startling even amongst this greenery.

"I'm Dylan. Pleasure to meet you, Lucy." He holds out a long sinuous hand. I shake it and stare.

"Who put you up to this? Was it Angus?" Jonny and Gregor Simpson's brother is a practical joker of some renown.

"Excuse me?"

"The costume." A silver embroidered black silk sleeveless tunic with heavy black silk trousers, mirror-finished black boots and silver wings. The creature, Dylan, frowns.

"Come on." He hauls me to my feet. "We must be off. Everyone is expecting you."

I've had enough surprises for one night, but nevertheless, "Hey, Dylan, wait for me," I pant as I try to catch him, but he's too far in front.

So far in front his feet aren't touching the ground. I stop and rub my eyes. Nope, definitely aren't touching the ground. I look down to make sure my feet are touching the ground. Only where my feet should be are grey leathery hoofs. I stop so abruptly I skid on the muddy ground. I raise my hands in front of me. I scream and scream and scream.

"Could you stop doing that? My ears are starting to bleed," says Dylan as he floats back towards me, wings fluttering.

"You're…oh my god…that's not a costume," I say.

"No."

"Then you're a…"

"Faerie. Yes."

"And I'm an…" The words lodge in my throat as my hands lift to feel my face. They can't quite get there. There is a trunk in the way.

"Elephant, yes. Now that's all sorted, can we get on?" Without concern, he hurries off again.

I chase after him. I'm really not sure how I'm managing it, but I pursue on four legs.

I have no idea where I am, except that I am scrambling through a forest. There are tall silver birch trees interspersed with ancient oaks, all bare but for a few newborn leaves. The low afternoon sun flashes between the trees as I dash past. My eyesight is still off, everything is so bright; the colors have a depth and clarity I've never seen before, almost crystalline. My feet should hurt as they crush broken thorny branches beneath them, but I feel nothing. A slow burn invades my calf muscles. I haven't used them properly in years. I'm sure I was wearing pigtails the last time they moved this quickly.

Dylan glides effortlessly in front of me. When he isn't whistling he is acting as tour guide, but I can't hear him over my ragged breathing, pounding heart and the thundering of my feet as they strike the ground, and when he stops suddenly I crash into his back. We both go flying, landing in a heap. The required breaking distance of three tones of mammal at full gallop is obviously longer than that of an overweight schoolgirl. I groan inwardly. *Way to go, Luce – why do you always have to be so clumsy?*

"She's arrived, as you can see," announces Dylan, jumping up and pulling me to my feet.

I turn my head slowly. We are in a circular clearing

surrounded by silver birch trees. I count thirteen standing like sentries guarding a temple. I close my eyes and open them again. I blink several times in rapid succession. Nothing changes.

For the second time tonight or whatever time this is, I have landed in the middle of my worst nightmare: me, center of attention, surrounded by people. This time they aren't yelling "Surprise!," but all of them are looking directly at me, some whispering to their neighbor, some tittering, most staring at me in stony silence. I quickly realize there isn't a human amongst them.

There are some that resemble Dylan in features, but with different coloring. There are some that have a human resemblance, taller less angular, but they have pointed ears. There are others that scary doesn't even begin to describe. Mountainous hairy creatures and little balls of fury that I definitely want to keep on the right side of.

I try to breathe, but my lungs have gone on strike. My legs give out. *What's happening to me? I can't...breathe.* I don't know if the words escape my mouth or not but next thing, through my haze, I feel a hand gently stroking up and down my back and an angelic voice in my ear.

"That's it, in...and...out," soothes the voice, and my taut muscles relax.

"Well done." I turn my head and stare. My jaw drops. "Quite an entrance," teases the voice. "There is no need to panic, Lucy. You are safe here. You will come to no harm."

"Umm," I manage.

"Let me introduce myself. I am Queen Imogen. Welcome to the Flowerlands."

Standing in front of me is the most beautiful being I have ever seen. She is very like Dylan, lean and angular. Onyx hair hanging to her waist. Silver moonshine skin and eyes the color of sun-drenched amethysts. She is wearing a white ankle-length antique gown; Grecian, I think. Her wings are fine platinum gossamer and her head is adorned with a crown of snowdrops and ivy.

None of this is what makes her beautiful. It's, well… there is a presence about her. She radiates light. It's almost palpable like the glow that surrounds a lantern. She exudes serenity, an infectious tranquility. I have to put my hand over the center of my chest as my eyes well. I have never experienced anything like it; it's like being with an angel or God or something. Otherworldly, purer than me. She lightly strokes my cheek, catches a tear on the tips of her finger and smiles gently at me.

"We all know why Lucy is here. Now that she is, let the festivities begin," she announces to the crowd.

With a couple of ear-splitting shrieks a fiddle starts playing a furious jig, joined quickly by another fiddle, a flute, a drum, a tambourine and two soul-searing singers.

"Come," says Imogen.

"Why am I here?"

"Later, Lucy. First you must try the banquet. It has been prepared in your honor."

I follow her to a fallen tree that has been sawn in half to create tables. It's a good job it is already on the ground as I can almost hear the mighty oak groaning under the weight of the feast upon it.

"Go ahead. You must be ravenous," says Imogen,

gesturing at the food. I quickly look from one side to the other but I can't see where to begin. No one else has touched the buffet.

"Umm..." My eloquence astounds me. My stomach gives an earth-juddering rumble.

"I'll go first, shall I?" asks Imogen.

"Yes, of course. Good idea. As queen you must go first. I insist." Imogen raises an eyebrow. *Oh do shut up, Lucy.*

I watch as Imogen picks up a wooden plate. I nearly trip over her heels in my haste to follow. As soon as I pick up my plate a long line forms behind me, snaking its way around the clearing. Everyone carries their own plates and spoons. I copy Imogen and take only small amounts. My trunk wrinkles as I approach each new dish. It smells delicious but looks far from edible. It's too healthy.

There are massive cauldrons of stew. Venison, wood pigeon and rabbit, the antlers, feathers and furry foot giving the contents away. I take a bit of venison, the others are a step too far. There are mounds and mounds of green leafy stuff. I take enough to be polite; I'm sure that much chlorophyll is poisonous. I err on the side of moderation in all things healthy.

I follow Imogen and sit on a tree stump at the edge of the clearing next to what looks like her throne, a high-backed wooden chair decorated with snowdrops and ivy. Dylan plonks himself on the ground next to me and proceeds to chatter between mouthfuls. I watch dancers laughing and reeling as I spoon food into my mouth.

Dylan finishes his food and jumps up and crooks his arm.

"Shall we." My eyes go wide.

"*Err*, I need to let my food digest." I don't dance as a human. How am I supposed to dance as an elephant?

"Suit yourself." He shrugs and turns to Imogen. "Your Majesty? Care to show them how it's done?" He bows and holds out his hand, and the Queen blushes and gives Dylan a beautiful smile as she takes his hand. He flushes bright red as he leads her to the dance floor.

The queue for food has dwindled so I head back for seconds. Checking no one is watching, I fill my bowl to the brim and shovel it down.

The sun has set and faerie lights have come on. I marvel at them twinkling on and off in time with the music. I giggle as I realize they are dancing dragonflies. Long torches have been thrust into the ground to illuminate the clearing.

The fiddles are picking up the pace; people are spinning like dervishes. They miss colliding with each by millimeters. My cheeks begin to ache with my polite refusals to dance.

I get up and hide in the shadows of the clearing, just watching. There are families sitting on blankets at the edges of the trees, grannies and grandpas, mothers with babes in arms, fathers bouncing toddlers on their knees, playing clap-a-clap-a-handy. Children are chasing each other, weaving in and out of the trees, darting through the dancers. Couples wander hand-in-hand through the privacy of the trees. There are groups of young men sipping dandelion beer and whiskey, teasing groups of young women who are whispering and giggling. Occasionally they pluck up the courage to ask for a dance.

I smile as a shy young man digs in his heels as his friends push his shoulders and taunt him. He surrenders and makes an "alright, I'm going" gesture, before asking a pretty girl to dance. His friends cheer as she takes his arm.

My smile slips and fades as my eyes lock with a pair of blue eyes so startling that I can tell the color from the other side of the clearing. I gasp and my heart speeds up as I take in the rest of the demi-God staring intensely at me. His straight hair is deeper than jet-black. It's the color of the end of the very last universe or the deepest of black holes, only shiny. He's solid; all muscle without being built. Lashes so long they should be illegal on a guy.

"There you are," calls Imogen serenely. She links my trunk with her arm, winding it around as if it were an arm and leads me forward. Of their own accord my eyes swivel for another peek at dark and dangerous. I sigh and my shoulder sags a little. He's gone.

I am introduced to hundreds of different creatures. There are faeries of all shapes, sizes and colors. The flower faeries are the brightest, dressing in a wide spectrum of colors. Their hair ranges from the traditional black, brown, blond and white to vibrant reds, greens, blues, yellows and purples. Their skin moves from silver-white to ebony and everything in between.

The pixies are a little larger than faeries and dress in browns and greens to camouflage themselves in the woods where they protect the animals. The hobbits are smaller and rounder and, I learn, like to dress in the colors of the trees they look after, anything from silver to brown. I am introduced to mountainous trolls that make me feel petite – large solid creatures composed of slabs of muscle, who like to dress in the colors of the stones they work with, greys, charcoals, beige and the occasional pink. The elves bear the closest resemblance to humans in features and stature. They are the makers and doers. Their clothes are usually linked to their industry; some colorful and some drab.

"Traditionally," explains Imogen, "faeries looked after the flowers, pixies the animals, and hobbits the trees, trolls worked with stone and elves made and built everything. I modernized when I became Queen and implemented what you might call an equal-opportunities program so we can be whatever we want regardless of our race. It's been slow to change. Most fae folk still follow in the footsteps of their forebears."

"What about them?" I yawn as we pass the group that dark and dangerous was standing in earlier. They are dressed in black from head to toe, exactly the same clothing as Dylan who is standing in amongst them laughing and joking when he isn't watching Imogen.

"The Protectors. They are my guards. They look after all of us."

Imogen catches the yawn I was trying to hide and leads me out of the clearing.

CHAPTER THREE

I arch my back and stretch my body awake. Sun is streaming through the window next to me. I am in the most comfortable bed I've ever lain in. The mattress is like a cloud below me, the sheets are soft enough to be silk and the comforter and quilt are like a hug from my grandmother, cozy and warm. I'm too comfortable to get up. I snuggle back down into the bed's warm embrace and prepare for a lazy morning.

"Good morning."

There goes my long lie. "Imogen, you scared me! What are you doing here?"

"Waking you up."

"What time is it?"

"Time you were up. Come on, we have things to do."

"No, really; what time is it?"

"We are not human. We don't run our lives by the hands of a clock. We have the sun and the seasons. If you want to know what time it is, look out of the window." Imogen parts the pretty curtains.

"The sun is still low in the sky. There's still a chill in the air so the sun hasn't been up long enough to heat the earth.

There is a mist low to the ground that hasn't been burnt off yet. So I would say it's about five o'clock in the morning, human time," she says. "Meet me downstairs when you are ready."

I sit on the edge of the bed and take in my surroundings, trying to clear the barely-morning fog from my brain. I am in a little wooden room. My bed is made of white painted wood with a heart carved out of the head and the foot. There's a three-legged table at either the side, one with a white ceramic jug filled with water. A little wooden heart is tied to the handle. Not sure what else to do, I stick my trunk in the jug and drain the contents. There is a fireplace laid with wood; a painting of bluebells hangs above the mantle. I kneel on the bed and open the curtains with my trunk. The window is an irregular shape, like it's been made to fit an existing hole. I make my bed of pink satin sheets with a lemon comforter adorned with white roses to match the curtains and a patchwork quilt in yellows, pinks, whites and greens. On the wooden floor is a large woolen rug in the shape of a daisy, white with yellow center. I glance around as I open the bedroom door and find myself smiling. It's all very twee, a million miles from my chic boutique-style bedroom at home.

I exit into a wooden corridor. The walls are like plywood, pale with the grain exposed; the floor is bare wood. The only light comes from low-burning wall sconces, and I don't know which way to go. There is no one about to ask for directions.

My eyes adjust to the gloom and I spy a wide curving wooden staircase. Holding onto the thick rope balustrade,

I descend into a vast cavernous space. Two huge multi-colored stain-glass doors shaped like a pair of wings face the bottom of the staircase. Holding open one of the doors is a large blond fae man dressed all in black.

"There you are," says Imogen, breaking off her conversation with the man, who I assume by his clothes is a Protector.

"I would have been here sooner if you had given me directions," I mutter under my breath. The Protector's eyes bore into me. I begin to shuffle uncomfortably under his scrutiny.

"Go on. I'll be there shortly," says Imogen to Mr. Intimidating. I'm relieved he has gone.

"Where are we, anyway?" I say.

"The faerie castle," says Imogen as we step outside into the sunshine. When we've walked a little way I turn to look back, gasping as I take in the massive oak tree that must be hundreds of years old. Imogen tells me that all of the flower faeries and some of the other fae live there during winter.

"Where are they now?" I ask.

"I expect most of them are in their beds sleeping off last night," laughs Imogen. *Lucky them.* "When spring comes, the flower faeries move out of the castle to their flowers. First the snowdrops, then the daffodils, and then the bluebells. The bluebells will be up in a week or two."

We walk through the trees to where the ground is carpeted with woodland flowers so small and delicate it's easy to overlook them. I've probably done just that on the few occasions Dad's dragged me walking in the great outdoors. I inhale a lungful of damp earthy air. It's so pure that it overloads my system and I get light-headed. *Moderation in all things healthy* I think, slowing my breath.

We come to the grove where the banquet was held last night. All signs of partying have been cleared away including the large logs. There are about thirty assorted faeries of all colors and sizes, twenty or so Protectors and a man and woman dressed in white flowing robes milling about quietly.

"What's going on?" I say.

"Just follow on," says Imogen as she floats away.

She sits crossed-legged the center of the clearing. The white robed man and woman sit either side of her and everyone else sits behind. Imogen is already completely and utterly serene. It doesn't seem possible to be that motionless and still be alive but I can see the gentle rise and fall of her breastbone. The others are all doing the same thing as Imogen. I look round. Dylan, trying to slip in unnoticed, puts his finger to his lips, floats to the nearest silver birch tree and sits down silently with his back propped against the tree facing Imogen.

I follow suit, feeling somewhat like an elephant in a china shop. At least I don't seem to have disturbed anybody. The sun is rising rapidly and slants through the trees creating a mystical light all around. The mist graciously rising in response to the sun's warmth accentuates the effect. My trunk begins to twitch, itching for a paintbrush and canvas to capture the magic.

Just when I think I'll explode if I have to sit still any longer, Imogen looks up and smiles. Everyone else comes to at the same time. They all stand and move around, hugging each other in some weird cultish bonding ritual.

My body stiffens when Imogen comes over to hug me but I manage to awkwardly return the embrace. I check over her shoulder and exhale loudly. The tension ebbs out of my body as I watch the others wandering out of the clearing, thankfully without hugging me.

"What were you doing?"

"Praying and meditating," says Imogen.

"Oh." *Do people really do that?* "What for?" My face screws up in confusion. I know I'm being rude. I can't seem to help myself.

"Well, myself, our priest Brother Michael and priestess Sister Sapphire and the others come and pray for all sorts of different reasons. For help with a problem; better health for themselves, relatives or friends. For something they would like in their life, a new job or a new home, a romantic partner or help with something they want to let go of."

"What do you pray for?"

"Me? Well, firstly I give thanks for all the good in my life, all the good in my kingdom and all the good in the world. I mostly pray for peace. I pray for good health for the entire kingdom. I pray for prosperity. I pray for the flowers, the bees and for the trees to stay healthy. I pray that the lands stay unpolluted. Many things."

"Huh." I look down at my paws. *In for a penny.* "What do you need to meditate for?"

"After I've prayed, it's nice just to be still. Not thinking about anything in particular. Clearing my mind, I calm and recharge and set myself up for the day from a positive peaceful place. Sometimes the answers to a problem will pop into my head when they've been given a bit of space to be heard."

One last thing. I have to ask. "Why do you have to be up so early?"

"I don't need a lot of sleep but mostly people are still asleep when I begin, so the energy is very still. It's quieter. I can hear the Divine more clearly at this time."

"*O-kay*."

We are still standing in the clearing when Mr. Intimidating comes up behind Imogen and whispers in her ear. She inclines her head.

"Take Dylan or Connor with you on your outings for the time being," he says, not quietly enough.

"Will do, Commander." He bows and turns away, not before glaring at me. I am relieved when a whistling Dylan enters the clearing swinging a basket.

"Thank you, Dylan," says Imogen so graciously I remember she's a queen. "Shall we breakfast by the river?"

We walk from the silver birch clearing on a meandering path through the trees. I have to admit, it's truly beautiful at this time in the morning. Dew is dripping from the grass and the branches. The birds are chirping away, pretty loudly it has to be said. There are a few snails lazily sliming their way across the path. The flowers are beginning to open themselves up as the sun touches them.

We leave the shadow of the tree and arrive at the riverbank. Dylan lays down a tartan picnic rug. Imogen sits and gestures for us to follow before she empties the hamper. There are several stainless steel vacuum flasks, hand carved wooden plates and mugs and a wide variety of fruits and nuts. I spot some muffins and load my plate with several of them. I regret my choice when I bite in and it's green.

Imogen and Dylan stick to fruit and nuts. They pour themselves tea and me a cup of coffee. When the others abstain I finish the muffins even though they taste earthy. I've managed six in all. I'm sure they are much smaller than the ones at home. It would be a crime to let them go to waste I think as I stuff the last one in my mouth, washing it down with another cup of coffee.

We sit for a while when we finish sipping our drinks. I stare at the clear pale green water gushing past. It runs fast from the snowmelt from the hills, the water singing as it hits the boulders, the noise soothing. I stare, transfixed. Even Dylan has stopped chattering.

"Why am I here?" I ask Imogen. I am so relaxed I sound drugged when I speak.

"Because it's your destiny."

"What do you mean?" Before she can answer, Mr. Intimidating comes out of the trees.

"If you're here for breakfast Lucien, you're too late. Lucy ate it all," grins Dylan, lying back with his hands tucked behind his head.

I feel the heat creep up my neck, but it's Dylan that gets the evil eye this time. He immediately sits at attention.

"Your Majesty, there has been an incident in the west woods that requires your attention," Lucien says gravely.

"Thank you, Commander," says Imogen, getting up gracefully.

"Do you need me to come with you?" asks Dylan, brows creasing.

"No. Take Lucy and show her to her room," commands Imogen. I'm seeing a whole different side to her, she's gone all kick-ass queen. Dylan does not look pleased to be babysitting me, but I didn't ask to come here.

"Let's go," he says striding off, hands in pockets, shoulders hunched. I fling everything into the picnic hamper and race to catch him up.

We stride through the woods, me panting, Dylan grumbling about never being allowed to do anything. It could be the same way we came this morning. It's hard to tell, it all looks the same. We eventually arrive at an oak tree. It's across from the faerie castle, which I do recognize. We skirt round the edges of the tree and cross a dirt-covered courtyard where the black-clad guys are fencing, wrestling, practicing hand-to-hand combat and some are sitting around in varying states of undress, cleaning and sharpening weapons or reading. My stomach flutters as my eyes do a sweep for a tousled black head. There's one, but he's short and stocky. It's not my day.

Dylan leads me into a different tree. He opens a hobbit-styled glass door and we enter a bright sunlight room. It's painted a chalky white and has windows on two sides.

"Your studio," says Dylan.

"Why do I have a studio?"

"To paint, of course."

I let out an attractive snort.

"I'm no artist."

"You sure about that?" Dylan cocks an eyebrow at me.

"*Pfft*! I've never painted in my life."

"Time to start, then."

I slowly spin round, taking in the room. "It's a great room."

Dylan grins and begins whistling. Nothing seems to bother him for long.

He opens another door that is hidden in the back wall and walks through. I follow. The room is hot and dark. I notice the fire at the end before I notice the naked sculpted back facing me. My mouth dries. Muscles are rippling down the sweat-soaked back as arms with bulging biceps and defined forearms hit something on a bench. I stare open mouthed and transfixed. This would be the perfect moment for me to experience cultish bonding rituals.

"Hey Connor," says Dylan.

"Hey," answers the Fire God.

He looks up at Dylan then looks over his shoulder. I gasp. It's dark and dangerous and he has a name. Connor. His name caresses my tongue as I whisper it. His eyes bore into mine before he gives me a brief nod, turning back to hammering a sword. It really is hot in the forge. I feel light-headed and a little breathless as I head outside.

CHAPTER FOUR

Dylan wakes me at ridiculous-o'clock the next day and we make our way to Imogen. Dylan is irritatingly happy, twittering away about what a lovely day it is, and how much he loves being up and at 'em. When he's not blethering away he's assaulting my eardrums with his whistling. I dawdle behind, bleary-eyed.

I thought I was a morning person before arriving at the Flowerlands. I was always up by seven on weekdays anyway, so that I could spend ages on my hair and barely there make-up, have breakfast and still have time to refine and review my Jonny fantasies before leaving for school. I guess I should change the hero from Jonny to Connor now. Obviously there is a starting point for my morning happiness, and it isn't five a.m.

We find Imogen and follow a trail through the woods, Imogen smiling indulgently at Dylan's constant chatter.

We arrive at a waterfall with a clear stony pool at the bottom.

"This is a good place for you to bathe, if you feel the need," says Imogen.

"Oh, OK." Tentatively I dip down and put a foot in the pool. *Brrrrr.*

Dylan starts a fire, while I'm directed to gather twigs and Imogen sorts out breakfast. She hands me a wooden bowl. I try not to wrinkle my trunk, but I can't help it.

"Something wrong, Lucy?" asks Imogen.

"No, nothing," I sigh. "Hmm, green things, yum," I say. I swallow the leaves as quickly as I can. Suddenly, green earth flavored muffins don't seem so bad.

"Maybe this will help," says Imogen, handing me a welcome mug of hot chocolate. *Proper food.* I sip slowly. I can tell it's been made with dark chocolate, creamy milk and cinnamon. I almost groan out loud with pleasure. Looking into the hypnotic flames, I feel comfort seeping into my bones.

"Why am I here?" I ask Imogen.

"You asked to come here."

"How can I have asked to come here? I didn't even know this place existed."

"You knew about us on an unconscious level."

"No I didn't."

"Yes you did. Lucy, you've been miraculously calm since you came here. Doesn't it feel a little familiar to you? Lucy, it was your destiny to come here."

"What are you talking about?"

"You made contractual agreement before you were born. We all do. We chose our parents, our parents chose us. We choose people who will be significant in our lives. We choose certain life lessons. We choose our purpose for this lifetime. You chose to be a messiah."

I choke as the hot chocolate goes down the wrong way. "Are you nuts? Are there mushrooms in your tea?"

"No Lucy," she sighs. "A messiah merely means a messenger, usually seen as having a spiritual message or a message from God. There have been plenty of well-known messengers like Moses, Mohammed, Jesus, Krishna, and Buddha. There are plenty of writers and *artists* who have shared spiritual messages. There are also messiahs on a smaller scale, like the person you sit next to on the bus who utters something that completely changes your perception."

"So, I'm supposed to be a messiah?" I scoff.

"There's no *suppose* about it. You're destined for it and if you weren't ready for it, you wouldn't be here."

I think for a moment, then smile. "Ok, then. Aren't you going to tell me this message?"

"Where's the fun in that?" replies Imogen in a heartbeat.

We start packing up the breakfast dishes into the picnic hamper. Dylan smothers the fire with earth, muttering some sort of thanks. I've noticed he does that a lot. Imogen walks off and I follow, leaving Dylan to carry the hamper.

We follow another woodland trail away from the waterfall clearing. This one is covered in autumn leaves that have rotted down over winter. They're nauseatingly squelchy under my feet. Imogen and Dylan start humming a melody in perfect harmony as we walk.

"Wow, you two sound amazing together."

They both gasp, cheeks burning and look everywhere but at each other. *What's that all about?* Imogen has stopped singing and Dylan is whistling. We walk on, my muscles beginning to burn. I've reached my lactic acid threshold and the sun is barely above the trees. Do we really have to walk everywhere – what about bikes? I start giggling. Seriously, an elephant on a bike?

Imogen and Dylan walk in front of me, stopping every so often to talk to the trees. I'm sure in my exercise-induced fatigue I'm imagining the rumbling responses. We cross a wooden bridge over a clear stream and enter another part of the forest.

These woods are populated by hulking great red pines. There is a thick carpet of pine needles that hide the treacherous ground underneath. The land is steeper and undulating with partially submerged boulders waiting to destroy my ankles. Sweat stings my eyes as I concentrate on staying in one piece. Imogen and Dylan are waiting at the top of a steep slope for me to catch up. It's easy for them – they just have to flap wings and float, avoiding the killer rocks. They are pointing in my direction looking concerned. Oh it's not me, they are pointing at some other trees now.

"Who set fire to the trees?" I pant as I reach them, wiping my brow.

"It wasn't fire but pollution that damaged them," sighs Dylan.

"How can people pollute trees away out here? I've only ever seen fae folks."

"Our energy is being diverted from caring for nature to trying to raise the vibration in cities and to counteract pollution, both environmental and energetic. Hence the disease," sighs Imogen.

"What's energetic pollution?"

"Fear, stress, worry," says Dylan. "If people could be

even a little grateful for what they have, it would make our job so much easier."

Imogen sends Dylan off to check the rest of the trees. She comes to my side and we amble on, the soft scrunching of the pine needles marking our walk. Finally we stop at the top of a stone precipice. The sun is high in the sky now. I can see for miles. The faerie castle's forest is below us to our left, with high hills behind. There is a plateau in front of us that leads to mountains beyond. There is a wide gushing river between the forest and the fields. To our right is the pine-covered hill that we just climbed. Water trickles down the hill somewhere in the trees nearby. We sit in silence for a while, soaking up the spring sunshine, listening to the stream gurgle, watching three buzzards circling overhead.

"To the North are King Andrew's lands; that's the mountains in front of us. The river runs between the mountains and the forest and leads to the sea in the west. That's Queen Fiona's lands. To the east just beyond the pine forest is agricultural land, King Garth's domain. There are four of us: two Kings and two Queens caring and protecting the earth and the fae folks," says Imogen, before handing me a leather pouch.

CHAPTER FIVE

"What's this for?" I ask, holding the soft brown leather.

"To collect your thoughts."

"And how do I put my thoughts into this tiny pouch?"

"Every time you have a negative thought you will pick up a stone and put it in this pouch."

"I don't have any negative thoughts."

"Really?"

"Really."

"What about when you say *I'm fat* or *I'm ugly*. Are these positive thoughts? Do you ever look in the mirror and tell yourself you are beautiful?"

I can't say what I'm thinking. She's being ridiculous.

"Well, you are, Lucy. Incredibly beautiful; you just can't see it. You look at yourself and constantly put yourself down."

"I don't!"

"You do. You look at yourself and belittle yourself. I'm ugly; I'm fat; look at the state of my skin; my hair is a mess, it never does what it's told. I hate these jeans, they make my butt look huge. I am huge. I hate my tummy, my bottom, my breasts, my nose, my eyes, my hair, and my legs. Ever said any of those things to yourself?"

"Well, yeah," I say, drawing my knees to my chin and hugging them. "Everyone does."

"You're right; a lot of people look in the mirror and find something to criticize about themselves. I'm too fat, too thin, too tall, too short. I wish my hair were longer shorter, black, brown, red or blond. I wish my eyes were bigger, smaller, blue, brown, green. I wish I had bigger/smaller breasts, longer legs, longer eyelashes. I wish my skin were black, white, brown, golden, tanned, darker or paler. Every time you say something like this you are rejecting who you are. Would you say these things to someone else?"

"Of course not."

"What if you looked at your best friend and said I will like you when you have lost weight, your hair is longer, your legs are thinner, your eyes are bigger, your eyelashes longer, when you have a tan, when your tummy is flat and your thighs are smaller? Then I can accept you as my friend. How do you think your friend would feel?"

"Not great," I say reluctantly.

"Yet you say these things to yourself."

"I'm OK with it really," I say, not daring to look at Imogen.

"So if I say to you, 'Lucy, you need to lose weight. You need to get your hair highlighted, your teeth whitened and false eyelashes. Nobody is going to want to go out with you looking the way you do. Definitely need to buy more fashionable clothes. You really need to exercise. You are so lazy. Not to mention stupid, even though you are an A-grade student, you still aren't clever enough. Nobody likes you, even though you've got two great best friends.'"

"You're horrible!" I yell, lumbering to my feet. "How can you say those things to me?"

"Why does this bother you? You say these things to yourself all the time. Why does it upset you when I say them? You treat yourself badly all the time. You constantly belittle and berate yourself. The way you speak to yourself in the mirror. The way you shrivel up around people, the way you hide yourself behind food. The never-ending stream of negativity."

It's all too much. Imogen comes and strokes gently over my hide. I want to push her away after all those ugly words but it feels so nice to be held and comforted. Eventually, after soaking through Imogen's dress, the tears subside.

"Better?" she asks, wiping the last of the tears away with her thumbs. "The anger and sadness you feel is good, Lucy. It means you are bumping up against your limitations. As Albert Einstein said, *once we accept our limits, we go beyond them.*"

We step off the stone outcropping and meander back to through the woods, keeping to well trodden paths to avoid crushing the flowering bluebells.

"So, every time you have a negative thought about yourself, pick up a stone and put it in the bag. Every time you think, *look at my hair, isn't it a mess* or *look how fat my thighs are* or *my butt is huge in this* or *I'm not healthy enough, I need to exercise more* or *I shouldn't have had that cookie* or *I have no self-control*, stone in the pouch.

"Moving a bracelet from one wrist to the other with each negative thought is another way of helping you become conscious of these thoughts. But I think putting a stone in a bag is easier with paws, don't you? Anyway, I'm going to leave you to wander for now and get to know us. Everyone is excited about meeting you, Lucy."

Dylan and I roam for a few weeks until I know my way about. Eventually, Dylan has to go and attend to the summer migration. The bluebells are already beginning to fade and the flower faeries are preparing to move from the spring flowers in the woodlands to the summer meadows, the big flat plains I saw from the outcropping. I miss him being around. He's always got something funny to say. I even miss his whistling.

As the days pass, I become more and more aware of my thoughts. At first I am picking up a few stones here and there. I only notice the big thoughts like, *Come on Lucy, can't you do anything right?*, *you are so stupid* or *you're a big fat clumsy elephant*. Then I start remembering all the times I said the wrong thing, all the times I did something stupid, all the times I embarrassed myself or someone else did that for me. Every little thing I've ever got wrong seems to have come back to me.

I am not enjoying this one little bit. I feel tired and drained most of the time, and it's got little to do with the number of stones I'm carrying. Imogen has provided me with a Hessian sack that sits at the main entrance of the castle. I've been making several trips a day to empty the pouch and the sack is filling at an alarming rate. I try staying in and around the castle but I soon use up all the stones. I need to go further into the woods.

It's a glorious early summers day and it's getting hot. I'm tired of all the trudging about. My body is weary. I decide to go down to the river and take a dip. I come across a gang of fae children all paddling in the sleepy river. Before long I am being splashed and I am hosing them all with my trunk. They keep climbing up my trunk to use it as a slide. The kids all leave as their mothers call them home for lunch. I climb out of the river and lay down on the bank. The sun beats on my skin and I smile, truly happy for the first time in … *well,* I can't remember. With contented exhaustion, I sleep.

A deep rich voice singing a haunting tune entices me out of my slumber. Lying curled up on my side with my head laying on my paw, I listen a while. The song is so dreamy I struggle to open my eyes. When I do, all I see is a black clad figure crouched at the edge of the riverbank. A head lifts and turns to look down river. I gasp as I recognize the profile.

"You're awake," says Connor, turning towards me. *Oh God, he's beautiful.*

"Uh huh."

"Imogen asked me to bring your lunch," he says, jumping lithely to his feet and grabbing the backpack. I watch as he pulls out a sandwich and hands it to me.

"Tea?" he says, pulling out a flask.

"Thanks."

He hands me a mug and sits down next to me with his own lunch. I watch him out of the corner of my eye as he chews his sandwich and sips his tea. He has lovely lips. My trunk tingles, wanting to trace their contours.

"Something wrong with your food?" he says, pointing to the sandwich getting squished between my paws.

"I'm not hungry," I say, just as my tummy lets out an enormous rumble.

"So I hear," he smirks. "Come on. You're obviously famished, and I made these sandwiches with my own fair hands."

"You did?"

"Uh huh."

I take a dainty bite of my cucumber sandwich. Hmm, it's deliciously simple and it's not entirely green.

"Do you want another one?"

"No, I'm good thanks." My stomach groans in confusion. *Well, that's a first!*

I watch as he makes his way through three more sandwiches and another cup of tea. He has an incredible appetite. I must be about two point nine tones heavier than him and I couldn't eat that much. *I suppose it takes a lot to feed all those muscles,* I sigh.

We head back to the castle in silence. He's definitely the strong silent type. I don't know what to say to him anyway.

He's gentlemanly, stopping to help me over logs or stones, not that I need it, but his hand touching me makes my tummy flutter.

"Well, thanks for walking me back," I say, blushing.

"It's my job."

"Oh."

My shoulders sag as I watch him walk away. *It's not like someone like him would be interested in me anyway.* I stoop to pick up a pebble I must have missed.

I enter the faerie castle and climb the stairs. I'm nearly at the top when I hear urgent whispering below me.

"You've seen them," hisses the Commander.

"Just keep them apart as long as possible," sighs Imogen.

"It would be easier keeping the North and South Poles apart."

"Please Lucien, she's making progress."

I stay in the shadows until their voices fade.

CHAPTER SIX

I head back towards the faerie castle at twilight surrounded by children. They usually find me at some point during the day. I tried to hide at first, but they thought I was playing hide-go-seek with them. I have several kids on my back, and others skip through my legs as I walk. I always wanted a brother or a sister but my parents were too busy to have more children after me. I guess this is making up for it.

The children scatter as Imogen approaches and leads me back to the grove where we banqueted on the night of my arrival. My feet stop moving when I enter the grove. There are hundreds of faeries sitting in a circle, and I soon see two are standing next to the sack filled with all the stones I've collected. Next to them is a low table covered in cloth with a candle burning, a stone, a feather and a bowl of water. Fire, earth, air and water.

All eyes are on me as Imogen leads me to the center of the circle.

"Lucy, this is Brother Michael and Sister Sapphire, our priest and priestess." Imogen gently pats my back before moving to sit between Lucien and Dylan in the circle. I am left alone with the two faeries dressed in long white robes edged with gold embroidery.

Sister Sapphire gives me a reassuring smile and guides me to sit with my back to what I think is an altar with the sack of stones in front of me.

"Brothers and sisters," says Brother Michael in a deeply soothing voice, "we are going to take Lucy's toxic negative thoughts and turn them into pure positive energy. Then we will release them and let them go. When you are ready, close your eyes and begin to breathe deeply."

I struggle to close my eyes, never mind slow my breathing down. I keep one eye open just to make sure that no one is about to tie me to the altar and stick a dagger through my heart. Sister Sapphire must be a mind reader. She leans over and whispers, "it's OK, Lucy, you're safe here."

I look around the circle. Everyone has their eyes closed and they all appear to be breathing deeply. They all look so peaceful. I can see, only barely, the Protectors standing at the edge of the trees. I let out a breath I didn't know I was holding. I close my eyes and begin to deepen my breathing.

"Now imagine that with each in breath you are filling your body with white-golden light and with each out breath you are breathing out white-golden light."

It's a bit of a struggle at first. What does white-golden light look like anyway? How do you breathe color? Several breaths later, my muscles begin to soften. My body starts tingling and then light starts coming out of me. Not just on my out breath, but it's like I can't contain the light any longer and it spreads outwards from my body until I'm sure I'm glowing. I peek around the circle again. I am possibly now certifiably crazy, because everyone is glowing with white shimmery light.

"Now that our bodies are filled with white-golden light, let's direct our out breath to the sack," says Brother Michael, who is sitting to my right.

OK, I can do this. Breathe in white-golden light and aim my out breath at the sack. In. Out. In. Out. The weirdest thing happens; within a few breaths the sack gets lighter. Don't ask me how I know. I feel the energy change from something heavy to something light. Kind of like when you take a wet sponge and squeeze the water out. When the sack is full and glowing, everyone comes to at once.

"We will take the sack to the river now," says Sister Sapphire. "The energy in the stones will help cleanse the whole river."

The Protectors come forward and lift the sack on to my back. Some fae walk in front of me and some behind. The whole procession is illuminated with flaming torches. Four Protectors walk on either side of me, including Connor, who doesn't even glance at me. The sack is lifted off my back when we reach the river. Still in silence, faeries come forward one by one gathering a handful of stones. They take it in turns to step into the river and release the stones. Some give thanks, some say prayers, others stay silent.

I am the last to go forward. There are more than a handful of stones left so I wrap my trunk round the top of the sack and drag it to the river's edge. I step down until I am in the water; I reach up to the riverbank and gather a paw full. I uncurl my paw under the water, letting the river take the stones from me. I do this several times until I turn the sack upside down over the water and the last few stones plop in. A great cheer goes up. Folks begin chatting and laughing with each other as they wander away.

I stay standing in the water, staring at the river flowing past. Carrying my past with it. I'm not sure where it leaves me. On one hand I feel lighter, freer but on the other I feel empty, almost sad.

"Are you OK?" asks Imogen from the riverbank.

"Yes, fine," I say. "I just need minute to myself."

"OK. Not too long. The celebrations are about to begin."

Once alone, I sink into the water. Before I know it great gulping sobs are making their way out of me. Minutes or hours pass. When the sobs subside I wash the tears away and lie back in the water. I feel great, about five stones – no, make that five thousand stones – lighter.

A torch has been left for me by the riverbank, and as I begin to climb a hand reaches for me. I look up into brilliant blue eyes, suddenly wishing the river would carry me away.

"How long have you been here?"

"I never left," says Connor. *He saw the whole thing?*

"Do you normally intrude on people's private moments?" I seethe.

"Don't be embarrassed. Even I cry sometimes."

"Seriously?"

"Sure." He shrugs, mouth lifting at the corner. *The Fire God has a sensitive side.* "It takes strength to be vulnerable. I always feel better afterwards. How are you feeling?"

"Good. No, great actually." His smile leaves me breathless.

We walk back to the grove, where the party is in full swing. There are tables groaning with food. The band is loud and fast. Laughter fills the air. Fae are standing about eating and chatting. Children skitter between bodies. Couples dance and jig. Connor and I stop at the edge. He stands beside me tall and elegant.

"Would you like to dance?"

"No thank you," I say hastily, surveying my paws.

"Suit yourself," he says curtly, striding off to join the other Protectors without a backwards glance.

I fill my bowl with a game and root vegetable stew and sit on a log by the dance floor. I try not to watch Connor as he laughs and jokes with his friends. With me he is mostly sullen and moody, and so I try to look aloof when he catches my eye. I watch Imogen flitting around talking with some, dancing with others. I wish I could do the same. Dylan charms everyone, even the trolls laugh easily with him and he dances with as many fae-women as he can, no matter how shy, no matter what age.

A sweaty Dylan plonks himself down beside me. "Not dancing?"

"No," I mumble, scuffing my hoofs in the long grass.

"Connor is a great dancer," he remarks.

I look up and there he is dancing a slow number with another Protector, holding a gorgeous red-haired faerie close. She's looking up at him in adoration, while he smiles back. *Yuck!* They make a stunning couple. Dancing must be another of Imogen's assigned duties. Thank God I didn't say yes. We would have looked like circus act. I can hear the ringmaster now: *'Roll-up! Roll-up! Watch in amazement as Connor the Magnificent does what no one else dare would dare to do. Watch astounded as he waltzes with Lucy the elephant.'* Ugghhhh! No thank you!

"What has Connor's dancing got to do with me?" I ask.

"I see the way you look at him."

"What do you mean?"

"Like you're a hungry lion and he's a baby gazelle."

"Yeah well, I've seen the way you look at Imogen."

"Imogen's my Queen, Lucy. I don't look at her any way but with respect," he says gruffly, getting up and walking away.

A lump forms in my throat as I watch a retreating back for the second time tonight. I make for the privacy of my room before anyone sees me cry again. I feel Connor's eyes boring me as I rush into the dark woods.

CHAPTER SEVEN

I dream my parents are at my bedside urging me to wake. My normally happy, laid-back dad sobs as my mum comforts him. 'Lucy's going to be OK, Mark. The doctors say the infection has gone.' His voice is scratchy. 'What if she never wakes up, Kate?'

I sit up with a start, my body dripping with sweat. I lean over and carefully take a glass of water between trembling paws. *What if she never wakes up?* What does that mean? Am I asleep? Am I going to die? I swing my legs out of bed. Time for some answers. The sun isn't even up yet but I know where Imogen will be.

I make my way through the gloom; the sky is overcast for the first time since my arrival. The grove is busy this morning. I spy Imogen, Dylan, Brother Michael, Sister Sapphire, twenty or so Protectors and a few dozen other familiar faces. I sneak in at the back and try to sit still until everyone is finished. Imogen is accosted immediately with community concerns. I shuffle my butt along the ground until my back is leaning against a silver birch tree.

"Morning, Lucy."

"Connor." I frown. *Gah! Why did I have to gush?* He comes

sidling up to me and leans casually against the tree, arms crossed, black combat boots crossed at the ankles, looking down at me as I pull up long strands of grass. "I didn't expect to see you here."

"It's part of being a Protector. We need to be pure in mind, body and spirit. Meditation and prayer is part of that."

"Like a Samurai warrior?" My tummy dances as I gaze up at him. Black just-out-of-bed hair, lightly tanned skin, bright topaz eyes, and sculpted lips just right for kissing. My face heats.

"More Samurai, less warrior."

"You don't fight?" My brows shoot up.

"We learn to fight so that we can defend ourselves if we have to and to stay in peak condition." He's definitely in peak condition. "Mostly we keep the peace and protect the land."

"Hey you guys! Where did you two get to last night?" Dylan asks, sauntering up to us. "Did Connor here sweet talk you into going for a walk in the deep dark woods?"

"No," I squeak. "I left *alone*."

"Connor here left straight after you *alone*, heading in the same direction," smirks Dylan, slapping Connor on the shoulders. I look at Connor.

"You followed me?" My jaw drops. He left redhead for me?

"I had to get back to the barracks. I was on night duty." He's fidgeting.

"Lucy left long before midnight," grins Dylan. "And as your night duty is sleeping outside Lucy's door…"

"WHAT?" I screech.

"I'm a Protector, I protect." He gives an unaffected shrug as color slashes across his chiseled cheekbones. If I could fold my arms I would. I stare at him.

"How long have you been sleeping with me?"

"I didn't realize I was." He smirks a crazy beautiful smile as he retreats. Turning, hands in his pockets, he saunters off.

"Lucy, what a lovely surprise," smiles Imogen, hugging me at the end of meditation.

"Am I dead?" I snap as she releases me.

"No."

"Am I going to die?"

"Well, of course you are. We are all going to die sometime. What's this about?"

I tell her about my dream.

"It's complicated," sighs Imogen. "You are betwixt and between. Your body is still in the human world. Your spirit is here with us in a different shell."

"So, how do I get my spirit back into the human world?"

"You transform yourself," says Imogen, gliding off.

I lumber after her.

"What do you mean *transform myself*? I'm already a bloody elephant!"

"A very beautiful one too."

"I WANT TO GO HOME." Everyone in the clearing turns and stares at me as I scream, including Connor.

"You shall in time. Let's walk to the summer meadows."

Huffily, I resign myself. There is no point pushing Imogen. She answers when it suits her.

We walk in silence to the edge of the forest and then onto the flat plains. The woodland flowers are drooping and shedding their petals. In contrast, the summer meadows are rife with tender shoots of possibility. There are faeries everywhere, standing around in groups chatting, practicing dancing, singing atop flowers, lazing back sunning themselves on leaves. The woods were tranquil and quiet; the meadows are vibrant and lively. I trail behind Imogen as she stops and chats with folk. I smile politely and answer questions until my cheeks ache.

We reach the end of the summer meadows, where they lay in the shadows of hills and the river bends between two mountain ranges. There is no one left to accost Imogen with concerns or good wishes or good humor. We sit at the foot of a heather-covered hill beside the river.

"Have you heard the saying *abracadabra*?"

"Kids say it all the time. Aladdin, right?"

"It's from the Aramaic saying abra-al-habra, meaning *as I speak I create*. Our thoughts and words shape our world. Every thought we think and every word we speak creates our reality. The universe is *always* listening and the universe *always* saying YES!

"When we have negative thoughts like 'life is crap' or 'nothing good ever happens to me' or 'I'm ugly' or 'I'm fat' or 'I'm not good enough', guess what we are going to get? We are going to get a crap life where nothing good happens where we feel ugly and we get fat. And don't get me started on Not Good Enough. If you feel that you are not good enough or don't deserve the good in life, guess what? You're not going to get it! So many people think they are unworthy of deserving good that they push it away, unconsciously of course.

"For example: you might be out shopping one day see a really pretty dress and fall in love with it. Consciously what you say to yourself is: that's a fab dress, I love it, I am going to buy it. Unconsciously though, you are saying to yourself that's a really fab dress, I love it but it will look hideous on me. If you bought the dress and wore it, you would feel uncomfortable because you unconsciously think you look awful in it. People will notice because you will be pulling on the hem or the neckline, looking uncomfortable.

"Instead, if you look at the same dress and think that's a really pretty dress, it will look good on me, it's my size and the color is perfect for me, I'll feel wonderful wearing that dress. Guess what? When you put that dress on you will feel wonderful and people will notice you feeling confident and good about yourself and they will be attracted to that.

"A belief is only a thought you keep thinking. Let me say that again. A BELIEF IS ONLY A THOUGHT YOU KEEP THINKING. That means that if we change our thoughts, we change our beliefs and we *change* our reality. Thoughts are like old riverbeds. The water, or in this case our thoughts, will follow the old riverbeds until we create new ones. If you want to feel differently about yourself or have only good things happen in your life, then you need to create new riverbeds that lead the water *or your life* in a different direction. This can take time. It's not an instant transformation. Your thoughts will want to follow the same old riverbeds, it's comfortable and it's what you know. You will have to consciously lead the water down the new beds towards a new reality. That's where positive affirmations come in."

I have to ask. "What are affirmations?"

"An affirmation is a declaration, a statement of intent if you like. We are affirming all the time. I'm stupid, I'm clumsy, I'm too tall or too short, too fat or thin, I'm ugly, I'm poor. I don't have enough money. I can't get a boyfriend. I hate my job. I don't have any friends. My family is a pain. These are all affirmations, pretty negative ones. When you use affirmations you are saying to the universe, this is my reality. So by choosing to say positive affirmations you are choosing to tell the universe that you want a different, *better*, life experience. So try saying I am beautiful, fit and healthy. I am enjoying studying a subject (or subjects) I love and will pass all my exams with ease. I have a job doing what I love which pays me well. I am in a fun, loving romantic relationship. I have lots of supportive friends and a thriving social life. I have enough money to pay all my bills and have fun. This is what you are asking for. This is what you will get. Oh, hello Dylan," beams Imogen as Dylan blushes. "Lunchtime already?"

I lift my head. Dylan has joined us with another picnic, and so we move from the shade of the hill to a sunny spot on the bend of the river where Dylan has laid down a tartan rug. He loads up three plates with fresh baked bread and butter, cheddar, apple, pickle and salad with bottles sparkling elderflower water. After all the woodland stews I've been having for dinner, this simple lunch feels positively decadent. We polish it off and Dylan pulls out bona fide faerie cakes complete with glimmering faerie dust. I pick a yellow iced faerie cake covered in rice-paper daisies, whilst Dylan takes a dark chocolate iced cake with toasted nuts and Imogen selects a lavender iced cake decorated with tiny silver flowers.

"These cakes are so cute," I say, licking the last of the icing from my lips. "Where did you get them?"

"There's a bakery in the village," says Dylan, before swallowing a mouthful of cake. "You should get Connor to take you. His brother Joe the baker makes the faerie cakes. I'm sure he'd be happy to introduce you."

"What a great idea, Dylan," says Imogen.

As I finish my cake, my body grows languid from the heat of the sun or maybe the faerie dust. Imogen and Dylan discuss matters of state whilst I doze.

"Lucy, are you ready to get on?" asks Imogen.

"Mmm?" I mumble, trying to wake up. "Sure, whatever."

Dylan and Imogen pack up the hamper whilst I get on to all fours and stretch like a contented cat. We follow the river, which edges the summer meadows, back to the woods.

As we reach the tree line, Dylan bids us adieu and veers off towards the castle. Imogen and I stroll on together until we reach a wooden bridge that spans the slow-moving river. We stand in the middle, both of us leaning on the handrail looking down into the water. The dusty smell of a hot day fills my nostrils as the breeze wafts gently past.

"Over the next few weeks you are going to concentrate on creating new riverbeds. As before, every time you have a negative thought about yourself you are going to pick up a stone but before you put the stone in your bag, you are going to replace the negative thought with a positive one about yourself. Give me some examples of the thoughts that have been coming up for you." My stomach immediately clenches and my lunch wants to escape.

"Come on, Lucy. I have a fairly good idea of what they are." I breathe deeply and puff out a breath.

"I'm stupid," I mumble.

"Are you?" I'm treated to the imperial brow arch.

"Yes! Well, no. Not really. Um... I'm quite clever really." My cheeks start to warm.

"And that's something to be embarrassed about?"

"Yes. No. Maybe. I don't know."

"But you are. You are a bright intelligent girl. Be proud of your achievements. So let's see if you can form a positive affirmation instead."

"I'm not stupid?"

"The brain doesn't hear negatives so it doesn't hear the word not or won't. So if you say I'm not stupid, what your brain hears is I'm stupid. You have to think of what you would like to be instead. If you're not stupid, you would be…?"

"Clever? I'm clever."

"Great. How does that feel?"

"Better."

"OK, Lucy. Let's try another one."

"I'm fat."

"Is that true?"

"Unfortunately," I grumble, looking at the ground.

"So if you keep telling yourself you're fat, what are you going to get?"

"Fat!"

"Exactly. So what are you going to be instead?"

"I'm going to be thin!"

"Do you want to be thin?"

"Of course! Everybody wants to be thin."

"Do they? Why?"

"To fit in, of course. Everyone is trying to be super-skinny. Trying to reach the holiest of grails, to be a size zero. I mean, size zero – who came up with that? Who wants to be a zero in anything? Some of the girls in my class at school are existing on air and lettuce leaves or smoking or they are sticking their fingers down their throat and running a zillion miles a day to be a size six, never mind size zero! Who wants that kind of pressure? *Ugh.* Not me, that's for sure!" I huff.

"So you don't want to be thin after all?" grins Imogen.

"I guess not." I frown. "I don't think I could be, even if I wanted to."

"So, what *do* you want to be?"

"I want to be a healthy… and happy maybe. I guess it doesn't matter what size I am, I just don't want to spend my life stressing about my weight."

"That's a great place to start, Lucy. It's important to say affirmations as if you already have them. If you say I want, then that's what you'll get – the *wanting*. If you say I'm going to, then you will always be going to and your wish will remain somewhere in the future. When you are creating your affirmations, you are creating your world how you desire your world to be. Always use I AM or I HAVE, in the present tense. Say it as if you have already become the person you wish to be, living the life you desire. Act as if you are clever, act as if you are a healthy body weight and it will happen that much quicker. Try your affirmation again."

"I AM happy and healthy. "

"You're doing brilliantly, Lucy. Give me another negative affirmation. Give me another one."

"I'm ugly." My eyelashes immediately coat with moisture. I turn my head away from Imogen, so I don't disappointment in her eyes.

"I *am* UGLY," I wail over my aching throat. "Nobody is ever going to love me."

Imogen swipes her thumbs under her eyes. "Let's think of something better than I am ugly."

Looking at the ground, I shake my head. "I can't. I just can't think of anything."

"That's OK. Sometimes it's hard to come up with something different than what we are used to saying. It's OK to ask for help. Let's try this: I AM BEAUTIFUL EXACTLY AS I AM."

"I am beautiful exactly as I am."

Yuck.

CHAPTER EIGHT

I dedicate myself to the task of becoming an A+ positive thinker. It is easier than I expected. I don't have quite as many negative thoughts as I used to and I dealt with the worst ones with Imogen, so that's made it easier. I have to pick up fewer and fewer stones and they are infused with positive energy before they go in the bag, so no cleansing ceremony necessary.

"Hi Lucy." I look up from where I'm covered in dirt, kneeling on the ground. His black hair shines blue in the sun. His chest is bare and glistening with sweat. Every last vein, sinew and muscle is pumped up and mouth-wateringly displayed. His chest is heaving from exertion.

"Oh, hi Connor," I say, unintentionally breathy. He pulls his shirt from the back of his trousers and covers up. Just as well, I was about to start drooling. "What are you doing here?"

"Running." He crouches down next to me, so that we are centimeters apart. Now I smell him. Clean sweat, woods and fresh air. Irresistible. My body sways towards him. "What's this? I've seen them scattered all through the forest." He points at the ground, inspecting the mosaic I have been making with twigs, leaves and my collected stones.

"Huh?" I clear my throat and command my body to inch back. "Oh it's nothing. I'm just mucking about."

"It's not mucking about, Lucy. It's art."

I blush as my tummy backflips at his praise.

"Imogen said to do what I like with the stones. I guess I should try drawing." My trunk scrunches up. "I don't have any supplies so this is the next best thing."

He looks up from the pattern directly into my eyes. My mind empties and I stare. "Maybe I can help you out?"

"Help...with what?" I can think of a few things.

"Supplies," he laughs. I sober instantly.

"That's OK." His face falls. "Thanks for offering though."

"Come to the forge in the morning." I open my mouth to tell him no. "It's starting to get dark. Why don't I walk you back to the castle? I'm heading that way anyway."

"Don't you want to finish your run?"

"No, I'm good. I've run twelve miles already." That explains his physique.

We walk back to the castle in silence. Every time I try to initiate a conversation he shuts me down with a one-word answer. I get a curt nod and gruff goodnight when we reach the huge winged doors.

I wake the next morning dreading the day. Connor was so surly yesterday. One minute we were laughing and the next he barely looked at me. It doesn't help my mood that I had another dream about my parents. This time my dad was singing Nirvana songs to me like he did when I was a little girl.

I get up, grab half a dozen morning cakes from the kitchen counter, well they're more like rocks than cakes, solid and full of mineral goodness with some dried fruits to make them edible. I wrap them in a linen cloth before putting them in a wicker basket. I'm sure Connor will manage several. The day is cold and wet. I forget my trepidation as I see smoke funneling from the chimney. I nearly take the door from its hinges in my haste to get warm and dry. Connor looks up from the fire and arches his brow.

"Sorry," I say sheepishly as I tiptoe round to close the door.

"I'm nearly finished. Have a seat."

I put the wicker basket down on the wooden table and sit on a stool at the end. I silently watch as Connor's arm muscles flex and strain as he lifts a hot cast-iron pot from the fire and pours molten metal into a thin rectangular mold.

"What's that?"

"It's steel." He takes a black lump from the workbench and puts it in the pot he's just poured the steel from and replaces the pot in the fire.

"What did you just put in the pot?"

"Iron ore." His back is to me as he stares into the fire.

"What's it for?" It's like pulling teeth trying to get answers out of him.

"Sword-making."

"Oh," I say. I'm not asking any more questions. Why did he invite me over if he didn't want to talk to me? I close my mouth and fidget as I wait.

"I'm smelting iron. Some metal I leave as iron and pour into these molds." He points to more rectangular granite molds. "Some I put in a hotter fire so that the iron becomes carbonized and turns to steel."

"You're a blacksmith?"

"Swordsmith," he corrects.

"Aren't you a Protector?"

"I'm both. Sword-making is one of my responsibilities."

"So how do you make a sword?"

"Watch—"

He takes two molds and casts out cold metal rods. Connor points to both the iron and steel. He takes the iron rod and heats the metal before hammering it into a sword shape. Explaining as he works that a sword has iron at the center because it is a softer metal than steel, which is necessary so that there is some give in the sword when it hits a target.

After the iron rod is shaped he blends steel round it. I watch as he coats the rod, adding extra steel to the tip and the edges for strength. I'm completely mesmerized as he finishes the shaft then adds a handle, explaining as he places the sword back in the fire that once the sword is shaped he will quicken to harden or temper to soften the metal depending on the swordsman's preference. The blade moves in and out of the fire as he works. He then takes the blade to a grinding stone turning it scarily sharp before polishing and oiling the now gleaming weapon.

"And there you have it, a sword." He is animated for the first time since I have met him and it's devastating.

"Wow," I sigh adoringly. "You are really talented." He just shrugs his shoulder.

"Coffee?" He moves a bubbling coffee pot from a small stove. He reaches to a shelf above the stove, grabs two mugs and puts them on the wooden bench before filling them.

"I brought breakfast," I say, handing over the basket. I am at ease as we munch and sip away, no embarrassment eating with him this time. "Have you been making swords for long?"

"All my life." he says, swallowing his third cake. "My dad was the swordsmith. This was his forge. He taught me everything I know. Times have changed since his day and we don't have use for a full-time swordsmith anymore. I make a few swords and daggers each year. Repairs the rest of the time. I get to make more artistic pieces now with there being less demand. And some folks want decorative or ceremonial swords, usually so blunt they wouldn't cut butter."

"So how did you end up as a Protector?"

"Even as a little kid I dreamed of being a Protector. That's all it was until Imogen changed the law. I was only twelve when I gained an audience with her and pleaded with her for an apprenticeship. My Dad was training me to take his place. Imogen knew there wouldn't be a full-time job for me and agreed to my apprenticeship and that was that. What about you?" He leans against the bench and crosses his arms and his shirt pulls tight over his broad shoulders and chest. "What do you want to be when you grow up?"

"Hmm? I'm going to university to study psychology next year. Well, that's if I ever get out of here." The thought overwhelms me.

"Are we that bad?"

"No, of course not. I just miss home," I sigh.

"Come on. I've a surprise for you."

He pushes himself off the bench, holds out his hand and looks down at my paws. He drops his hand quickly before walking away. I hop off the stool to where Connor is standing at the door to my studio.

"Ready?" He grins boyishly, puts his hand on the door, pushes it open and steps back.

"OH MY GOD CONNOR!" I move to the center of the room, slowly spinning in a circle trying to take it all in.

The studio was bare when Dylan first brought me here: nothing but white walls, wooden floors, large windows and amazing light. There is a large wooden easel in front of a window with a blank canvas resting on it. There is a smaller easel and small canvas to its right. There are dozens of blank canvases stacked under the right-hand window. Against the back wall are a large wooden floor-standing cupboard and a wooden table. I stroll over and stand in front of the large easel. The light is perfect. I run my trunk over the top of the large canvas, then the small easel, then over the top of the stacked canvases until I'm in front of the cupboard.

Inside there are five shelves. The deepest shelf is at floor level where there are two large metal canisters with black writing on them. One reads *turpentine* and the other *linseed oil*. The next shelf holds clear jam jars currently empty. The next shelf holds lots of little clear glass jars with metal lids, about the size of pots of my favorite moisturizer. The next shelf holds the same again, only the jars are double the size.

I close the doors and look at the table. There is a jam jar tied with twine around the rim with a rose quartz crystal heart tied to the twine. It contains ten pencils. I pick them up, every grade I need for sketching including HB, 4B, 2B and the rest, an eraser, metal sharpener and a sketchpad. There is even a leather satchel to put it all in. Next there is a piece of Hessian. I undo the ties and roll it out and gasp. There are at least thirty horsehair brushes with worn smooth blond wood handles.

"It's too much." My voice shakes as do my hands as I reach out and tenderly caress the brushes. "I can't believe you did this."

He shrugs nonchalantly. "It was just stuff that was lying around."

"Thank you," I say, feeling Connor's face heat as I impulsively kiss his cheek.

CHAPTER NINE

A few days later a summer storm has kicked up. The wind was gale force in the nighttime, I hardly got any sleep between the howling and broken branches clattering against the window. The wind has died down this morning and torrential rain has replaced it. No way am I going out picking up stones today.

Instead, I fly down the stairs, not bothering with breakfast, hurry out of the door into the battering rain, slip over the forecourt, skid round the back of the barracks and make a dash for my studio.

I courteously enter through the forge, rather than my private door, to let Connor know I'm there. The fire is burning but nobody's home. I warm my trunk and paws in front of the fire and stay there until I've chased the chill away. I pour a mug of the coffee from the pot and take it into the studio. I am a little deflated. I leave the studio door open so that the heat from the fire can warm the studio. Not so I'll see Connor the second he comes in.

The carpenter who made my mixing pallet kindly agreed to cut me some round pieces of board. I got a hold of some plaster of Paris and some glue and I have been using my positive affirmation stones to make mosaics. I even managed to get some old pieces of colored glass, broken china and tiles from this cool reclamation yard.

I'm putting the finishing touches on my third mosaic when Connor comes in. Water is running off him and pooling on the flagstone floor. He takes off his black wax jacket and leather boots. Stands on one foot to peel sopping wet socks from his feet, opens the forge door and wrings them out outside.

He looks at me and grins. "I think I need to change."

Above me, I hear the thump of feet, a drawer slamming shut, the creak of bedsprings, then nothing. I stand in the middle of the forge staring at the ceiling. I shake my head to try to clear my thoughts of Connor and his bed and move to refill my coffee and pour a cup for Connor. He comes down in jeans and faded blue shirt, barefooted. It's the first time I've seen him out of uniform.

"Something wrong?" He catches me staring.

"No, um. I didn't realize the fae wore jeans."

"It isn't the dark ages, Lucy. Just because we chose to live differently from humans doesn't mean we aren't aware of your society. We even have computers. How else can we get up to mischief on the internet?" He winks, taking the mug of coffee I am holding out to him. Wow! I had no idea.

"Would you like some lunch?" he asks.

"Is it lunchtime already?"

"Way past lunchtime."

"Really? I haven't even had breakfast yet."

"Me neither," he says, opening the door to a cold store.

"My brother has left some soup and a loaf of bread. Fancy it?"

"Sounds good." On cue my very empty tummy rumbles. Connor pours the soup into a cast iron pot with an over-handle, hooks it onto a metal arm and swings it over the fire and sits down yawning.

"Were you up early this morning?"

"No, I haven't been to bed yet."

"What have you been doing?" I freeze as I wait for his answer.

"Clearing carnage, re-homing folks, you name it I was doing it," he says through another yawn. "We lost a few of the ancient trees and they need to be cleared away. Some folks lost their houses when the trees toppled. Faeries had to come in out of the flower fields to be put up in the castle for the night. There's quite a lot of damage to the flowers and a lot of upset fae who are taking it out on Imogen. What about you? What have you been up to?"

"Making mosaics. Hold on." I hurry to my studio and back. "I made this for you." I hold out a dark earthy circular mosaic, all greens, gold and blacks with the occasional fleck of blue.

"Nice!" he says, staring at it. He gets up and puts it on the mantel above the fire. He swings the pot out of the fire, pours two bowls of soup and slices the fresh baked bread.

"What is it?" I ask, frowning at the green liquid in front of me.

"Wild green and garlic soup. It's my favorite." *In that case!* I pick the soup-spoon up with my trunk.

"Oh, it tastes much better than it looks," I say, taking a mouthful.

"What are your plans for this afternoon?" he asks, between hungrily scooping up his soup.

"Well, I've run out of stones so I thought I might grind some of the crystals down to get ready to mix into paints."

"Need a hand? I'm experienced." When he sees me flush pink he adds, "I used to help my Mother do it all the time."

"I wouldn't mind an experienced pair of hands helping me grind." I turn so red I'm practically glowing. "With the rocks, I mean."

We banter lightly as we work away together. Connor grinds the stones into fine powders with consummate ease, whilst I fill and label the jars. The hematite is the last, powdering into a vibrant red.

"All done," I say as I close the cupboard door and wipe the table clean with an old towel.

"You've missed a bit."

"Where?" I look round. The table and the floor are spotless. He pushes his butt off the edge of the table and takes the towel from my hand.

"Here," he steps right up to me. He lifts the towel and wipes my forehead. "And here." He moves the towel to my left cheek, so gently it's practically a caress. I look at his eyes as they drop to my lips. "And here," he whispers as his thumb caresses my bottom lip. My lips part. His eyes never leave them and then his head lowers towards my lips.

"Hut hmm." We both start and spring apart. I turn to find Dylan grinning manically in the doorway.

"Not interrupting anything, am I?" He waggles his eyebrows at us.

"We were just tidying the studio," I say.

"Oh really?" Dylan smirks.

Connor clears his throat. "Did you want something?"

"Lucien requires your presence," says Dylan. Connor, raises his eyebrows when Dylan just stands there.

"Immediately,"

I hear Connor banking the forge fire as Dylan gives a slow whistle as he spins in a circle.

"I like what you've done with the place." I grin delightedly at him. "Fancy going out on the town with me tonight?" says Dylan. Connor halts in the doorway, giving a curt nod before striding out.

CHAPTER TEN

The café is on a busy tree-lined avenue. It is the main hub of the Flowerlands. There are shops down both sides of the street. Most are housed in trees with apartments above, sometimes more than one level. There are some stand-alone shops built between trees. The shopfronts are built out of the front of the trees, almost like conservatories. We arrive at the bottom end of the street walking side by side. Dylan is patient as I stop and look the shop windows.

There are a lot of shops. There's a hardware shop, a corner shop, a butchers, a fruit and veg shop. We pass the pub where a band is playing and a great murmur of conversation drifts from the closed doors. Then there are the artisan shops: a soaperie, candlestick maker, and a craft shop. There is an interiors shop with cushions, woolen blankets, woolen rugs, bedding and little trinkets like the ceramic jug I have at the side of my bed. There is a furniture store where the majority of very unusual shaped pieces are crafted out of wood: beds, chairs, tables, wardrobes – you name it, it's wood.

There are a few different dress shops. A children's clothes

shop, a shop full of bright high performance work clothes, a shop for casual clothes and a shop that looks to be selling haute couture. I stand gaping at the exquisitely tailored suits and formal dresses until I spy Dylan giving the red head Connor was dancing with at the last banquet a wave. I quickly tug his arm and pull him away. We stroll past a few more shops. Lots of folks stop to say hi and chat with us but there are others that walk past oozing animosity.

The bakery café is in the center of the street, and even in early evening seems to be the center of the community. The sky is dull and grey even though the rain has stopped. There is a curving walkway leading to the front door. The path is lined with cottage garden flowers giving off a sweet scent, subtle enough not to interfere with the alluring smell of fresh baked bread. The shop is in two halves, each with its own black lacquer door. One side is the bakery with its curved glass window with Georgian panes. Adjoining it is the café with a floor to roof glass front. The bakery is brightly illuminated whilst the café side is lit softly with the flicker of candles.

There are hanging baskets dripping with trailing flowers, four in all, one each side of each window. There are planters full of bright colored flowers. It's inviting. I plaster myself against the bakery window to ogle the display. There are baskets full of loaves of bread all shapes and sizes. There is a shelf of cakes: ginger bread, tea bread, lemon drizzle cake, coconut macaroons, chocolate fudge brownies and red velvet cake.

But what have really got my mouth watering are several cake stands of faerie cakes. They are pink, blue, purple, red, orange, lemon, white and chocolate colored cakes with mind-blowing decorations: everything from rice-paper daisies to sugar-crafted woodland and summer meadow flowers. There are caterpillars and disgusting bugs and spiders and butterflies so well made I'm not sure if they are actually real. There are cakes that look like the faces of trees.

"Wow, these are amazing."

"I'll let you into a secret." I spin round at the sound of Connor's voice. "They taste even better than they look." I look around me then up and down the street. I frown.

"Where's Dylan?"

"He had to go." He was here twenty seconds ago.

"Why would he leave? He's been droning on about how much he's looking forward to dinner since we left the castle." Connor saunters to the bakery door.

"You coming?"

Without waiting for a reply he turns the handle and steps in.

"Be with you in a sec," booms a voice.

"You'd better be! I'm dying of hunger here," calls Connor. A head pokes around a door at the back of the bakery.

"Connor!" The booming voice is matched with a bear of a body. A tall Thor impersonator grabs Connor and squeezes him in a death-like grip before releasing him and slapping him on the back. I wince at the noise.

"Good to see you, Joe," grins Connor. "Have you met Lucy?"

"No, I haven't had the pleasure," smiles Joe charmingly, coming to where I'm still plastered against the wall to avoid the Viking Invasion. "Good to meet you, Lucy." He squashes my paw with his.

A petite Goth-like violet-haired faerie appears, bustles over to me, takes my hand and thoroughly digs her fingers in to check for broken bones. "It's all that hefting sacks of flour and mixing bread."

"Sorry," says Joe.

"Anyway, good to see you," she says, before wrapping Connor in her delicate version of a bruising hug. She only seems a little older than Connor but her manner is definitely maternal.

"Lucy this is Joni, my sister-in-law. And the big guy here is my older brother Joe."

"Nice to meet you both. I see the resemblance now. Same blue eyes and bone structure."

"Not so much on the body. I take after our da and pipsqueak here takes after our ma," say Joe, playfully punching Connor in the arm.

"So, what can I do for you two?"

"I was hoping we could get fed," says Connor.

We are led through the opening between the bakery and the café. The café is decorated in much the same way as the bakery. The floor is wooden. There is tongue and groove pearl white paneling to midway and then two walls are painted a pale lavender and two violet. Booths have been formed with the same tongue and groove. Grey, turquoise and violet tartan seat cushions line the benches and there are various cushions in matching tartan and silver, purple and turquoise velvet strewn over the bench. The tabletops are wooden, with decorative iron legs. They each have a glass jar of lavender, thistles and babies-breath tied with purple ribbons and a tea light. There are pendant lights hanging from the ceiling to save the interior being too dark.

As we walk into the café the effervescent conversation dies and people stare. I slide into the booth at the opposite side from Mr. tense and moody.

"Connor," I whisper, tentatively touching his hand. He finally looks up at me. "We don't need to stay if you're embarrassed to be with me." I look down at the table.

"Why would you say that?" He frowns. "I don't care what other people think, Lucy. Let's just enjoy our dinner."

"Here we are," says Joni, handing us two pieces of slate with the menu written in chalk before pouring two glasses of water from a jug she places on the table.

"I'll take the special please, Joni." As there is only one item on the menu.

"Me too."

"Coming right up," she says, before hurrying off.

"You have got to be kidding me." I'm gob-smacked.

"What?" says Connor, looking confused.

"Are you telling me that I have been eating bowls and bowls of green leafy things and vegetables and mushrooms when all these weeks I could have been having pizza?" I hiss. "Seriously?"

"It's pizza night." He shrugs as if that explains it.

An awkward silence descends which Connor quickly fills with a bit of family history.

"Joe's my one and only sibling; he's five years older than me. No nieces or nephews, not yet anyway. We lived above the forge. Dad died eight years ago; mum three months later."

"How awful! How old were you?"

"I was twelve. It wasn't so bad for me; I got to join the Protectors. It was worse for Joe. He was left holding down the forge. Still, when I graduated he finally got a his dream job and eventually married his dream girl."

"Do you have a dream girl?" He stares at me fleetingly before looking away.

"Yes."

"Hi Connor." I turn my head to find the red-haired Protector standing beside our table, looking at Connor as if he's an item on the menu.

"Tatiana!" He smiles at her. "Have you met Lucy?"

She eyes me coolly. "Not yet."

I take her proffered hand in my trunk, sorely tempted to give it an extra hard squeeze. She turns her back to me and leans her hip against the table, devouring Connor. "Are you coming to the party tonight?"

He looks at me and shakes his head.

"What a shame," she all but purrs. "That's what you get for volunteering to babysit," says Tatiana.

WHAT? Connor's face turns the color of Mars. My jaw hits the floor. Our eyes lock.

"OK then. Guess I'll see you later..." Tatiana's eyes narrow as she takes us in. "Or not." She runs her hand over Connor's shoulder as she sashays to the next table.

Two other Protectors join her. A whippet-lean blue-haired female faerie and a male elf that might be half wolf. They are as both beautiful as Tatiana. No wonder folks hardly fight, they probably give themselves up just to spend time in the Protectors' stratosphere.

"What about you?"

"Huh?"

"Do you have a boyfriend?"

"Umm..." I'm not sure what the etiquette is of explaining a possible boyfriend in another world to the guy you're hot for in this world. "Maybe? I kissed a guy the night I came here. I don't know if it was a mercy mission or if there's something to go back to." I shrug, not wanting to admit how much I care about Connor's reaction.

He gives nothing away, and I find myself jabbering away about my parents – anything to fill the space.

"Dad's an architect, mum an interior designer. They run a business together. Dad works *all the time*. Mum socializes all the time. Mum jokes that she's just the mistress and dad's real wife is work. He's handsome and charming, she's vivacious and beautiful. Nothing like me," I sigh.

"Oh I don't know." My head jerks up. I search his face.

"Here we go," says Joni, placing one huge pizza in front of us. "Sorry it took so long, it's a mad house in here tonight." I groan in ecstasy with my first bite, savoring every morsel of hot goo and comfort.

As we finish Connor excuses himself to have a word with Joe.

Conversation from Tatiana's table reaches me.

"I mean, have you seen her? " says Miss Whippet.

"What was Connor thinking bringing her here?" says the wol-elf.

"And Imogen agreeing to it!" counters whiney-Whippet.

"Guys!" Tatiana forcefully interrupts, jutting her chin in my direction. Both whip round.

"Oops," says the big-bad-wolf. I want the ground to open and drag me to the center of the earth.

When my muscles unfreeze, my body jerks to standing. The water jug smashes on the floor.

"Lucy?" comes Connor's concerned voice from the bakery.

"I have to go," I croak. I accidentally shove Connor in my haste to get away.

"What did you do?" He seethes as I dart out the door. "Lucy, wait!"

My feet have a mind of their own and begin to gallop. My lungs are on fire and my muscles burn as I race frantically to God knows where. I stumble several times, banging my shoulder against a tree. I barely miss running into other trees, swerving at the last minute, in the gloom of the deepening twilight. When I trip over a tree root and just miss hitting my head off a boulder, I decide to halt. I pull myself to sitting, rest my back against a broad oak and drop my head to my folded-up legs. This is how Imogen finds me.

"Are you alright?" Imogen asks as she floats down to sit next to me.

"Fine," I mumble, head still buried.

"Connor told me what happened." Her voice is gentle.

"They were horrible." I lift my head. Angry tears

threaten to fall. "They don't want me. The faeries don't want me. My parents don't want me." Unwelcome tears pour silently down my cheeks. "What am I doing here? Why did you bring me here?" Imogen turns her head from me and looks out into the forest.

"I am to prepare you."

"For what?"

"To change the world."

"Me?" I'm on my feet, vibrating with anger. "I didn't ask for this!" I yell.

"Yes, you did," says Imogen, glacial in her calmness.

"But I'm a nobody. I'm nothing. How am I supposed to change the world? I can't even change myself!"

"You will change the world," says Imogen, coming to place a gentle hand on my cheek. "You have already begun."

CHAPTER ELEVEN

I smirk as we pass the Protectors' training ground and Lucien is barking orders at three familiar Protectors doing press-ups in the mud. When Imogen and I arrive back at the faerie castle, Connor and Dylan are anxiously pacing in front of the main door. They immediately assume nonchalance. Dylan escorts Imogen inside and I am left to face Connor.

"I'm sorry—", "Are you—" we say at the same time.

"You first," he says.

"I just wanted to apologize for running out on you earlier." I'm still too embarrassed to look him in the eye.

"Don't worry about it. I just came to check you're OK."

"Who, me? Yeah I'm fine. I've only got to single-handedly save the planet, apparently. You know – no pressure or anything!"

"I'm sure if anyone can do it, you can."

I sigh and stare at the ground.

"I mean it, Lucy!" He steps in front of me and puts both hands on my shoulders, forcing me to look at him. "Just look at everything you've achieved since coming here. It would have broken a lesser elephant." I melt as he kisses me goodnight on the cheek before jogging towards the barracks.

The first thing I do when I wake up is touch my cheek where Connor's kiss is still smoldering. I throw back the covers, bursting to get on with the day. Rising at dawn doesn't seem so bad now that I'm floating on air. I wish everyone I meet an exuberant good morning, including the trees, the rocks, the river, the animals and the birds as I trot towards morning mediation.

I've timed it perfectly. Everyone is beginning to rise. Connor gives me a shy smile before Dylan captures his attention. I break into a crazy grin before bashfully looking at the ground. When I look up, Imogen is eyeing me speculatively.

"Ready to get on?" She is a queen on a mission. She has a brief word with Commander Lucien. She is polite but doesn't let anyone detain her. Lucien interrupts what looks like Connor and Dylan winding each other up. To my surprise, it's Connor that walks over to us. He lifts up a heavy hamper and we set off at a furious pace.

We head straight for Everest. OK, we are not in Nepal but this mountain is a monstrosity. I wonder if the hamper is so big because there are oxygen tanks in there? I thought my weeks of wandering woods and fields had got me fitter but my legs tire quickly on the inclines, all four of them. We take plenty of scenic breaks to let me catch my breath and wipe the stinging sweat from my eyes. My calves and hamstrings burn red hot as we climb from one blind summit to another.

The top is desolate. No humans, no fae, no animals and no noise apart from the wind. There are only jagged peaks covered in grass and boulders and us. A flat glassy loch the color of emeralds lies in the middle. Clear blue sky reflects on the water surface. The vistas of the lands below and beyond go on for mile after wondrous mile. I gape in open-mouthed amazement, slide the hamper off my back and let it drop to the ground.

"I didn't know you got lochs at the top of hills – and the color! I love the way it's emerald green in the middle and lightens to aquamarine at the edges. It'd make a great painting."

"You can bring your paints tomorrow," says Imogen.

"Tomorrow?" I squeak.

Connor lays out a selection of fruits, nuts, woodland greens, doorstopper sandwiches as well as a selection of mouth-watering cakes and a flask of tea. We eat with gusto, replenishing our energy stores depleted by the grueling climb.

"*Sooo*," I drawl, sated and contented. "Why did you bring me all the way up here?"

"We are here so that you can begin to see the beauty in yourself."

"What do you mean?"

"You can never be truly contented unless you are content with yourself. You can never be truly happy unless you are happy with yourself. You can never truly love another unless you love yourself. The only way to replace the emptiness and neediness that drives you to what I call *thingness*, the driving need to possess things in the hope of fulfillment, is not with food, alcohol, drugs, fashion, social media, having the perfect body, gossiping, gaming or whatever. It is with *LOVE*.

"Fill yourself with self love. Everyone is born filled with it. Babies love everything about themselves. They don't look in the mirror and berate themselves. They look in the mirror and are fascinated by how wonderful they are. As time goes by we learn to judge ourselves and find ourselves lacking and our self-love diminishes. It's a bit like being in a bad relationship with our self. We begin to believe all the negative comments and our self-belief and self-confidence erodes. So you are here today to begin to accept yourself exactly as you are. You are here to love yourself."

"Err, isn't that something I'm supposed to do in private?"

"Probably. If people saw you looking in the mirror telling yourself how beautiful you are they would probably criticize you. After all, most people *don't* love themselves. Often people try to sabotage us when we try to change, especially for the better as it upsets the status quo. So you might want to start by doing it on the quiet, behind closed doors."

"What was that you said about looking in a mirror? I don't do mirrors." Well, only briefly to avoid going out looking a disaster.

"You do now. The loch provides a flat mirror-like surface. You are going to look at your reflection and see yourself, I mean *really* see yourself, until you can tell yourself that you love yourself."

I jump up, heart racing, knowing what it feels like to be a cornered animal.

"I'll be right beside you," soothes Imogen, leading me slowly over the undulating grassy earth, all the way to the stony edge of the loch.

"When you are ready, I want you to look into your eyes," she says in a soft whisper.

I straighten my shoulders, inhale deeply and step towards the water's edge.

"Great Lucy, well done. Now, look into your eyes."

I lift my eyes from my feet. My eyes slowly graze my reflection until I am looking into my own eyes. After a few seconds that feel like eternity, I break eye contact and stumble back.

I take off like my tail is on fire.

I'm sitting on a rock next to a small waterfall at the end of the loch. My butt is numb with cold. I'm mindlessly throwing pebbles into a small emerald pool.

"I don't understand, Imogen. I've been doing so well. I've been really happy and feeling really positive about myself. Why can't I look at myself?"

"Several reasons. Firstly, we have different bodies: physical, mental, emotional and spiritual. We have dealt with your mental body, the way you *think* about yourself. When you undertake mirror work you are dealing with your *emotional* body. That's a whole different ball game.

"Secondly, you have spent your whole life denying what

your heart knows to be true – that you are beautiful. When you look into your eyes you look into your heart and your soul. You will no longer be able to deny your own beauty. Not only that, you will have to face up to the fact that you have denied the truth and lied to yourself all these years.

"There is a darkness that society controls you by – it's called repression. Denial of one's self is pervasive in the whole of society. When a child is born, is it accepted for who it really is?

"No, only what your society perceives as right or normal can be accepted and appreciated. As a child you have to work it out. You are smiled at if you get it right or you are frowned, shouted at or smacked if you get it wrong. So you learn to deny many parts of yourself; deny them so early on and so pervasively that you become completely unaware of them.

"When we look in the mirror we become our own judge. This can be frightening at first, as we can no longer deny who and what we truly are. We are all beautiful and we are all love. I know this might not make complete sense to you right now, but bear with me," she says when she sees me frowning. "The task of truly looking at yourself isn't easy; however the rewards for accepting yourself are great. To be one's true self is the greatest gift we can receive, if we are willing to accept it!"

"So, what now?" I blow out a defeated sigh.

"If at first you don't succeed..."

"But I couldn't do it, Imogen. I tried, really I did, but I couldn't. All I saw was this great big ugly elephant, which is what I always see in the mirror. A great big ugly me! Which isn't fair because I normally love elephants. Not when I'm one, though. Why is that?" I swipe at the tear rolling down my cheek.

"You've learned an important lesson today. In fact, I think you may have learned the most valuable lesson of all. It's not what is on the outside that matters but what's on the inside. Do you get it?"

"Of course I get it! It's what's on the inside that counts. Oh, OH, OH!" My thoughts scramble to rearrange themselves. "For the first time in my life, I get it. I mean I really get it! It doesn't matter what's on the outside. It doesn't matter if I wear designer clothes, make-up, highlight my hair, wax, buff or tone. It doesn't matter if I follow the latest fashion trends, the latest diet, if I have piercings or tattoos. It doesn't matter if I weigh eight stones or eighteen stones, if I'm a size six or a size sixteen. If I don't like what's on the inside none of that will matter. If I feel ugly inside, no amount of clothes or make-up or stuff will make me feel beautiful and if they do it will only be temporary.

"That's why I couldn't look at myself. Even though I adore elephants, I still couldn't look at myself even as an elephant because if I feel ugly on the inside, no matter what I do on the outside I will always see myself as ugly. It wouldn't matter if it was my human body or the body of an elephant or the body of the most beautiful woman in the world, I would never see beauty would I? That's why I couldn't look at myself, because all I saw was UGLY and I couldn't face it." I gasp softly as realization sinks in.

"Yes, and if you keep looking, eventually *all* you will find is beauty. You will know that ugliness is an illusion and you will only see beauty. That's all you have ever been, that's all you are now and that's all you will ever be: beauty-full, full of beauty," says Imogen.

CHAPTER TWELVE

We arrive back at the other side of the loch. The sun is high in the sky although the wind keeps us cool this far up. Connor is at the shore with a fishing pole staked in the sand and a line in the water. My heart contracts when I see him tense and hunched. He gets up and envelopes me in a bruising hug. It's a struggle to lift my trunk over his shoulder to pat his back. He holds me so long that I eventually relax and hug him back. Finally, he steps back.

"I wish you could see what I see, Lucy." His voice is jagged.

"Me too!" My eyes begin to well. "I'm sorry I upset you."

"That's the past. Are you ready to create a different future?" says Imogen.

"Definitely." I can do this. I *have* to do this.

"Good. I would like to try a different exercise before you go back to your reflection in the loch. OK, Connor and Lucy I would like you both to stand and face each other. It is important for this exercise that you stand with eyes level. It doesn't work if one person is higher and the other lower. Now, look into each other's eyes. Keep your eyes open. Keep facing each other. Look deep into the eyes of the beautiful person across from you," instructs Imogen.

My emotions are all over the place. My body wants to jiggle. I mean, this is totally ridiculous, standing staring into someone's eyes. How am I supposed to look into Connor's eyes? I have a hard enough time not embarrassing myself as it is. I could stare into his beautiful eyes all night over a candle-lit dinner for two, or in a dark corner of a club, but not here in front of Imogen!

Time distorts and slows down excruciatingly. Then, all of a sudden, something unlocks deep inside me. Standing before me is the most beautiful being I've ever seen. What's more, the feeling is mutual. I can see my beauty reflected in Connor's eyes. I can see how he sees me. I can see *what* he sees in me. Without warning, my heart bursts open, not in a nice way. In an unexpected incendiary device kind of way that is both messy and painful.

I crumple to the ground as years of pent-up emotion shudders its way out of my body and I begin to not just cry but also howl. I don't even have the wherewithal to be embarrassed even though Connor is watching. I'm in too deep. I've no idea how long it takes for the wailing to subside and tears to dry. When I come to, I'm in the fetal position, rocking to and fro on the beach.

"You cannot deny that you are truly beautiful when you see it reflected in someone else's eyes," says Imogen as she gently strokes my back.

"No, I can't." I laugh as I sit up, wiping my puffy eyes and snotty trunk. I notice Connor out of the corner of my eye rigid with tension.

"When you are ready, in your own time begin looking into your eyes," says Imogen.

I take a tentative step towards the water's edge, then step into the shallows. The gently lapping water tickles my toes. I stand still to allow the surface to calm. I take a deep breath and lift my head until I am looking myself in the eyes.

It feels awkward and unnatural. I look at the reflection of the sky, the clouds, the surrounding hills, and the birds chasing each other across the sky, anything but at myself. I release my breath with a defeated sigh. I keep looking at myself until a definite ping alerts me that I'm focused and truly looking at myself. Then it starts. Look how small my eyes are. *I've got a tufty bit and huge feet and …*

"What's going on, Lucy?" asks Imogen.

"Uh…, some internal chit-chat." I bite my bottom lip.

"All good, I hope?"

"Well…not really,"

"It's to be expected," assures Imogen. "Go back to looking at yourself and every time something crops up like *Look at my tummy* or m*y thighs are huge* or whatever it happens to be for you, just say to yourself *I am beautiful* and keep repeating that statement; use it like a mantra. In fact, I would like you to repeat it to yourself from now on – walking, sitting, painting."

I look at my reflection again, trying to do anything but look at my own eyes and hey presto, the elastic snaps and I'm looking at me. *Look at the size of my butt! Oops, I am beautiful* and after another little while *Look how wrinkled my skin is, where's moisturizer when you need it? I am beautiful. I am beautiful. I am beautiful.* On and on ramble the thoughts until I bring them to heel with my new mantra.

"Well done, Lucy. I think that's enough for today. Back to the castle now?" suggests Imogen.

"Um, What? Yeah. Sure." My brain has been replaced with marshmallow.

"Where has Connor got to?" says Imogen. "Connor," she shouts. "Ah, there you are."

"I'm good to go," grins Connor with boyish pride, pulling a large trout from behind his back and placing it in the picnic hamper.

We trek back to the castle. The sun is beginning to drop behind the hills. The sky is colored with beautiful soft pinks and lilacs with peach streaks closer to the sunset. I make a mental picture and file it away for a painting day. Imogen and Connor are deep in serious conversation a little ahead of me. I'm too buoyant to be affected with their tension. I must be quite light on my feet as some rabbits run and hop in front of me on the lower slopes. I spot several deer eating grass as we approach the tree line. They lift their heads but don't startle. They just ignore us, drop their heads and carry on grazing. The forest is suffused with a soft golden light as we wander through it. The birds welcome us home with their evening song.

Connor leaves us just before the castle. I can't help grinning when I see him showing off his trout to the parade ground.

CHAPTER THIRTEEN

I have developed a routine over the last few weeks. I hang about in bed as long as possible while Imogen is meditating. I grab enough food to feed an army or at least Connor or sometimes Dylan. Then we head up the monstrous hill better known as the Sleeping Soldier that I hope it never wakes up. The trolls in these parts are intimidating enough without a mountain wandering about.

Connor and I take our time climbing the hill, at least Connor does. I go as fast as I can, puffing and panting my way to the top.

"You're getting fitter," says Connor at the summit. Today is overcast. The weather has been amazingly sunny, unnaturally so. I'm used to a lot more grey days and rain.

"Yeah, I am," I grin. "Who knew exercise could be fun?" I drop my leather satchel to the ground and stretch. I notice my breathing has returned to normal already and I'm not nearly as sweaty.

"Oxygen. Endorphins. What's not to love?" Connor is one of those happy outdoors sorts.

"I used to go walking with my dad and my granddad when I was little. We would walk in country parks and sometimes hillwalking. It was fun I guess. Then dad got too busy and took up running." My trunk wrinkles. "That was then end of that. There's PE at school, presided over by a drill sergeant who has taken it upon herself to reward my lack of competitiveness and athletic ability with public humiliation. *Then* there's my mother who decided last year that I needed to get 'healthy', her way of saying I need to lose weight. So she got me a gym membership for my Christmas. Some present that was."

The memory flashes into my mind. First of January, mum and I side by side on treadmills. Snow on the ground outside the huge glass windows. Music pulsating. Mum sprinting away, beautiful as always, fully made-up, coordinated size six gym gear, not a hair out of place, not a drop of sweat gracing her perfect body. There I am beside her, puce and gasping, the treadmill barely above a walk. Resplendent in sweat-magnifying grey tracksuit bottoms, t-shirt big enough for a baby whale, clinging in all the wrong places, plastered to my breasts which are bouncing in directions that defy physics, magnifying my tummy's ample size, stuck to my back where you can now see through to my bra. Along comes Men's Health Man – all gleaming white teeth, natural-looking fake tan, Hollywood action-man physique including razor-sharp six-pack and washboard abs flashing his smile at my mum, then recoiling in horror when he sees me.

I am beautiful I say to the memory, and move over to the loch for my mirror work.

*

When I'm finished, we eat. Connor eats enough for five people and still he is all hard lean muscle. He lays back and fishes whilst I try to decorate some stones with indigenous style images. A couple of dots, a couple of lines, some swirls. It's infant level really. I finish my final dab of emerald paint and hold it up for Connor to see.

He takes the rock from me, twisting it to catch it in different lights. A smile spreads across my face. "It's for you," I say.

"It's about time!" My jaw drops.

"I beg your pardon!" Shock makes my eyes prickle with tears.

"Come on Lucy, you know what I mean. I gave you those paints weeks ago and you've done nothing with them." I gasp, trying to suck air into my empty lungs.

"Oh my god. You wished you'd never given them to me."

"What? Don't be absurd."

"Well, you can have them back," I say, thrusting the few jars of paints I brought with me into his arms.

"You're being ridiculous."

"*I'm* being ridiculous? Did it ever occur to you that it's ridiculous to paint with a trunk and these?" I yell, wiggling a paw in front of his face. "That maybe I'm being ask to do things that are so far out my comfort zone that I'm overwhelmed? That I'm in a world where I don't belong, where everyone resents me being here? Where they all have an agenda for me? That maybe I'm scared?" I poke him in the chest with my trunk, punctuating each statement like an exclamation mark.

"Of course it didn't. Mister Perfect has never been

scared in his life. Well, screw you MR HOT FIRE GOD. With your perfect body and your gorgeous blue eyes."

My eyes widen and I bolt down the hill when I realize what I've said.

I slam the door as I enter my studio. *Who does he think he is?* I take one of the canvases and thump it onto the easel. I grab a brush and a few jars of paint. I curl my trunk round a brush and open the first jar. I've blindly chosen cerise, orange, ochre and crimson. I start slashing paint across the material. The colors bleed and blend into each other. Finally, running out of steam, I sit back and look at what I've done. It's a mess of anger. Sighing I stash it behind the yet to be used canvases. I clean up and leave via the forge. Connor is missing and the fire is cold.

I poke my head round the dining room door when I arrive back. I'm surprised when I walk in to find Imogen in deep conversation with another female, at least I think it's female.

"All our Kingdoms need this. You don't have a lot of time. Why don't you ask him?"

"As Queen, if I ask him he has to agree. I want to know that he wants me for *who* I am, not *what* I am. Besides, Lucien has already offered." She looks up guiltily when I enter. "Where's Connor?"

87

"Not sure. Haven't seen him since this morning," I say casually.

"Oh?" She scrutinizes me.

"Hut hmm." Imogen's companion clears her throat.

"Where are my manners? Fiona, this is Lucy. Lucy, Fiona – Queen of the West and the Ocean." I lean over the table and hold out my left paw to shake her hand. She stands to take it and nearly crushes it.

"It's a delight to meet you at last," says Fiona, her eyes boring into me.

I thought I had gotten used to unusual in the Flowerlands, but Queen Fiona takes unique to a whole new level. Her snow-white hair that cascades down to her waist has aquamarine highlights throughout. Her eyes are sea green. Her whiter than white skin sparkles like the surface of the sea on a bright sunny day. It almost distracts from the intimidating Amazonian bulk of her body. A body that is encased in very tight electric blue leather. Second-skin trousers that draw your eyes to her bulging thigh muscles and sculpted claves. She wears a tight, tight zipped vest top that most of her Z-cup cleavage is playing peek-a-boo with. As she moves, very defined biceps flex and ripple. I stare, enthralled.

"Won't you join us?" says Fiona.

"Umm… I'm not hungry," I say, blushing. I feel Imogen's eyes on me.

"You'll be doing me a favor. Imogen has to see a faerie about a proposal and I'd rather not eat alone."

"Umm… I guess," I say, sitting down, unsure how I'm going to be able to eat in front of this intimidating creature.

Imogen bids us good night, gets up and kisses Fiona's cheek and give my shoulder a squeeze as she passes. I ladle the fish dish into a bowl and fill a chalice with rhubarb and ginger wine.

"So, what brings you to the Flowerlands?" I ask before spooning stew into my mouth.

"I'm arranging Imogen's marriage."

I choke at her words.

She gets up quickly and thumps me on the back. My lungs nearly come out my mouth. I take a gulp of wine to wash the food down but it burns and I splutter before screwing up my face.

"Why?" I ask when my throat is clear.

"Her birthday isn't far away."

"What's that got to do with Imogen marrying?"

"She must bear a child in her twentieth year or give up her kingdom. She must be married and pregnant by the winter solstice."

"That's ridiculous."

"That's Sovereignty. We fae are oath-bound creatures. We take our vows to serve our kingdoms very seriously. Our needs and wants become secondary to our kingdoms' needs and wants."

I stand abruptly. "If you'll excuse me your Majesty, it's been a long day and I'd like it to be over."

CHAPTER FOURTEEN

I take in the vibrant dichotic landscape. I'm Picasso's 'Girl Before the Mirror'. My blond hair, my profile, my circles for breasts, my full belly, my curving thighs, it's my hand reaching out of the embryonic reflection staring back at me. She reaches out a hand and pulls me through the mirror. *"Now I understand what you tried to say to me,"* she whispers.

When I step through the mirror I'm Dali's 'The Persistence of Memory'. I've never seen the paintings before but I *know* them. It's not a melting pocket watch sliding to the earth below – it's a two-dimensional me. The other pocket watches turn to me and chorus, *"They would not listen, they did not know how."* I'm falling fast. I look down. I gasp as I recognize Dali's 'Christ of St John of the Cross' from rainy Sunday mornings in Kelvingrove Art Galleries. I'm looking down at dark hair, hands nailed to the cross, body slumped forward almost wrenching arms from their sockets as he rises above the world. He looks up at me. It's not Christ's eyes that bore into mine, it's Connor's. *"They could not love you, but still your love is true,"* they seem to say. There is something familiar about the words, an old song maybe? I fall right past his beauty being extinguished in the most heinous of ways.

Straight into the Louvre in front of the most famous woman in the world. Mona Lisa smiles at me then stands. She morphs into my mum and starts banging on the glass between us shouting *"with eyes that know the darkness in my soul"*. I stumble back. When I turn Leonardo Di Vinci's 'Vitruvian Man' is advancing on me. One head, four arms and four legs. I cover my mouth with my fingers to catch the hysteria. "*Sketch the trees and the daffodils.*" I barely make him out over his thick Italian enunciation. I turn and run. A man looks up from the water lilies he's painting. "*Flaming flowers that brightly blaze, swirling clouds in violet haze,*" he mouths. I lift my feet higher and move them faster. It's not Monet's voice carries on the wind but my dad's.

I stumble to a holt in a landscape of swirling blues interspersed with circles of gold. I'm so taken with walking into 'Starry Night' that I hardly notice the bearded man walking towards me. He holds out his hand. The swirls drop from the sky and start whirling around me. "Take it," they whisper. I look down and scream at the ear Van Gogh is holding out to me. *"There's no hope left inside the starry, starry night."* He looks solemnly at me still offering his ear. I turn to escape but his sunflowers are closing. Where the black centers should be are the faces of the artists singing, *"We could have told you Lucy this world was never meant for one as beautiful as you…"*

They get closer and closer. The are suffocating me. I can feel myself fading. I scream. My body begins to waste away. I turn into Edvard Munch's 'The Scream'.

The sunflowers turn to me, "what else are you wasting away?"

I wake on a gasp. The sky is hinting at dawn. *What else are you wasting away?* I fling the covers back stopping in shock when I notice that the bluebell painting above the fireplace has been replaced by my unfinished 'River of Rage'.

CHAPTER FIFTEEN

I get to the clearing too late to grab Connor, for morning mediation is just beginning. Imogen smiles and takes her place. Connor blanks me. Dylan gives me a brief nod but doesn't approach. The Commander practically growls at me, as per usual. I take myself to the back, out of everyone's way. I manage to stay still, but the time drags in. I just want to clear the air between Connor and I. I corner him as soon it's over.

"Not now," he says sharply. Imogen asks him something and he nearly bites her head off. At least it's not just me.

"Connor and Dylan are needed here," says a harassed Imogen. "Hundreds of visitors are about to descend on us. With the butterfly festival only four days away it's all hands on deck."

"Can I help?"

"Yes. You can carry on your exercises by yourself; you should be safe for now. I've asked the kitchen to prepare enough food for you for several days. No point coming back to the castle. It will be mayhem around here." Someone else who doesn't want me around. "If you need help carrying the hampers, ask Connor." She hurries off.

I go to my studio before collecting the food. I notice the forge door is open. I give a tentative knock before I enter. I smile as Connor looks up briefly whilst continuing to sharpen a sword as I enter.

"Busy with the festival, huh?" Nothing. My smile vanishes. "Connor, I'm sorry about yesterday but you hurt me."

"I hurt you?" The sword clatters onto the stone floor. "Every day you are here hurts me."

What?

"Every day you waste your talent hurts me. Every day that you could be helping others hurts me, but you are too self absorbed to care." He is breathing heavily.

"I thought you liked me?" I whisper.

"Not at the moment."

"Well, I don't like you either," I yell.

"I have responsibilities that include more than babysitting a spoiled brat." I suck in a breath. "Don't you think it's time you made yourself useful instead of just taking everything for granted? Maybe give back to the community that is helping you? I've never met anyone so ungrateful." He picks up the sword at his feet and stomps around the wooden table to where I'm standing.

"What exactly am I supposed to be grateful for? Being kidnapped and held against my will?"

His face blanches. He stops in the doorway with his back to me. "Just so you know: if you don't hurry up it will be winter and we'll be stuck with you forever. Believe me, none of us want that!"

"Yeah, well, I didn't ask to come here!" I scream at his retreating back.

*

I make it up the hill in record time. I stomp around muttering to myself for a while before I fling myself down and start throwing stones into the water. With a sigh I take myself to the water's edge and kneel down. I look at myself. What do people see when they look at me? What does Imogen, Dylan or Connor see?

I can't stand to look at myself. I get up and start pacing. How dare he call me selfish! They've kidnapped me. Held me hostage. Demanded I *save the world* or something. Now they're all pissed at me because I'm not doing what they won't tell me I need to do. Who the hell do they think they are? I plonk myself down on the ground and throw open the lid of the first hamper. Grab a sandwich and another and then another.

The sun is setting by the time I calm down. I've emptied two hampers and three days' worth of food. No wonder I feel sick. I close the lids and stagger my way to a small cave in the rocks behind me. I crawl in on my hands and knees. The base is a large slab of granite. I sweep away some rocks, twigs and dust, lie on my side and start to bawl.

My mind floods with memories I'd rather forget. Mum's eyes dancing then going blank as I seethe, 'I can't believe you did this', moments after a light is thrown on in a darkened room. I am blinded as fifty shiny happy people yell 'Surprise!'

I float about and fake joy as everyone congratulates me. Even the popular kids from my class that don't normally have anything to do with me wish me a casual happy birthday. The fact that Jonny Simpson is there with yet another girl who isn't me doesn't help my mood either.

My Dad leads me over to a stack of mostly professionally wrapped presents. The ones that take forever to untie with some fancy-shmancy bow and unwrap paper that is too thick to tear. My face gets redder and my grin gets tighter with each present. Each present I open gets more expensive and more pretentious. Emotion suddenly overwhelms me; I burst into tears and run out into the back garden.

"What's wrong, sweetheart? Too much for you?" asks daddy, coming out and wrapping me in his arms. I see my mum over dad's shoulder, hovering at the backdoor, unsure of her welcome. He leans back and looks down at me. "You got some great gifts."

"No I didn't, I got some great one-upmanship."

"Pardon?"

"Oh come on, dad. Your friends gave me those presents so they look good. They're always trying to impress you and mum."

"Our friends *care* about us. They went out and spent their hard earned money on presents they thought you would like."

"Well, I don't want those presents," I shout. "All I asked for was a trip to Rome. You subjected me to this party even when I asked you not to…"

"I had no idea that your mum arranged this party."

"I don't care! Would it have been so hard to ask everyone to chip in for something useful, like the trip? It's the only thing I wanted." My eyes start to water again.

"We discussed Italy, Lucy. Mum and I are too busy to take time off..."

"You're always too busy." I scream.

"... and there is no way you are going to Italy on your own, you'll be barely sixteen," Dad says through gritted teeth.

"Three iPads Dad! What am I supposed to do with three iPads?" I yell.

"You're supposed to smile and say thank you. Is this who I've raised? A spoiled ungrateful brat?" Dad closes his eyes, then with a gravelly voice says, "I never thought I'd say this but right now, Lucy, I'm ashamed to call you my daughter." He walks away, putting his arm around mum's waist and leading her back into the house. A huge lump forms in my throat. It's so unfair! I make my way into the shadows at the bottom of the garden, which is where Gregor finds me.

One minute we were together about to count down to my birthday, the next I'm in this place. I didn't get to say goodbye to my parents. I didn't get to tell them how much I love them. I didn't get to say thanks for all the things they've done for me. Our lovely house they bought so I would have a big garden to play in. The bedroom they created because they wanted me to have somewhere special for me to be with my friends. The clothes they bought for me. The food they fed me. The seaside holidays at home and abroad. The trips to art galleries. To museums. The cinema. Shopping trips. Eating out. The time mum and dad took off work for my school concerts and class productions. Sundays with dad playing in the park and going for ice cream. Crazy days with mum.

They have done so much for me and I just expected it. Never thanking them. Expecting, never really appreciating. Connor is right. I am selfish. I am ungrateful. Overwhelmed and heartsick, the world dims to shades of grey and I climb into a dark place.

The tears come, dragging memories behind them. Dad's face red with anger at my party. Mum's eyelashes coated with tears as I lash out at her for organizing my sweet-sixteenth. Sitting in a church with the still, lifeless bodies of first my Papa, then my Nana, pine covered just feet away from me. Dad's shoulders shaking.

Asking dad for help with my homework. "Later Lucy, I've got to get this done," he replies, never taking his eyes from the computer screen. Same answer when I ask to go for a walk with him, for a ride to my friend's house, to go to the cinema, anything. Mum's heels clacking against the hall floor, bending to kiss my check. 'No sorry, I can't darling I'm meeting…" a client, a friend, your dad. I've been promised many tomorrows.

Lucien's many looks of frosty disdain. Connor's face stricken with horror at the Emerald Loch as I run from my ugliness. My stomach churns now as I remember what was reflected in the water. The sadness in Imogen's eyes as I tell her what I saw. Dylan's retreating back as he abandons me at the banquet. Imogen abandoning me for her duties. Connor's back rigid with tension when he tells me he doesn't want me anymore, walking out on me. A revolving door of people leaving, human and fae. Slam, slam, slam, slam, slam. Alone again.

I moan in pain. I'm a snake shedding its skin. Slithering over the rocky desert. Each stone tears another painful moment from me until the old is gone. Only the beautiful memories remain.

On dad's shoulders, strolling through the park, mum at his side, all of us laughing. Wet days and welly-boots, splashing in puddles with mum, both of our trousers soaked, twirling around and around as the rain drenches us. Sticky fingers, sticky mouth, eating cake mixture when Nana's back is turned. Papa's holding a nail whilst I hammer, pretending that I hit his thumb, plastic thumb falling to the floor. Sunday dinner dad and Papa trying to outdo each other's terrible jokes, me and my cousin Jamie cracking up, mum, nana and aunt Claire groaning.

Dad teaching me to ride a bike, I take off, flying free. Mum showing me how to put on make-up so as not to look like a clown, how to accentuate my eyes, plump my lips. First time my besties Daisy, Gordie and I were allowed out by ourselves, the nervous anticipation of entering the café and ordering our own hot chocolates. The three of us linking arms and striding through the front door on our first day in High School. Turning round in English Lit realizing that Jonny was no longer my childhood friend but my ultimate fantasy. Gregor walking me home from school day after day. The two of us sitting cross-legged on my bedroom floor moaning about chemistry. My first ever kiss.

Imogen's mesmerizing beauty, her serenity. So many gentle, loving looks given to me. Dylan showing me around.

Dylan's beaming smile as he laughs and jokes. The softness in his eyes as he tenderly cares for Imogen. Connor's smile. Connor's eyes. Connor, hot and sweaty in the forge. Connor helping me over rocks. Connor singing to me. Connor showing me the studio. Connor almost kissing me. Connor, Connor, Connor…

CHAPTER SIXTEEN

"Connor?"

I have no idea how long I've been in the underworld when I open my eyes. I am still lying in the cave. It's flooded with light and Imogen is beside me.

"Well hello there!" She gently strokes my brow, eyes creasing with concern. "How are you?"

"Fine," I mumble as I sit up. My mouth is dry and gritty, like my eyes. She hands me a water pouch and I gulp down the cool drink.

"Why are you here?" I'm groggy and confused.

"Connor came to get me."

"Connor?" *But he hates me.*

"He came to check on you. Eventually found you in here. He's been watching over you for the last three nights."

"Three nights!" I screech.

"I told him to come and get me when you started stirring. He's got a fire and some food waiting. I expect you'll be hungry."

She leads me outside and I wince at the bright morning. Connor is poking the fire with a stick. I rub my front paws together and hold them out to the fire. Imogen hands me a cup of creamy hot chocolate. I am grateful for the warmth.

"I thought I had died," I say into the fire.

Imogen turns to me.

"I'm... not sure how to explain it. I could hear mum and dad beside me talking about all the things we did together. Then my friends Gregor and Jonny and their little brother Angus all started speaking to me. I could hear them but they couldn't hear me.

"Jonny said, 'this is taking getting out of exams to the extreme, Lucy. You might miss the prelims but you'll still have to face the May exams. Hurry up and wake up, I need my study partner back.'

"Then Angus was telling me these really crappy jokes." I look up at Imogen and Connor. "Why did the mushroom go to the party?" Imogen quirks her brow. "Because he's a fungi!" Connor is stony faced and Imogen gives me a polite smile. "A fun guy, get it?" They just stare at me. "Then Angus just started crying and I could hear his mum saying 'it's OK love, Lucy's going to be fine.' Then Gregor, I could feel him taking my hand in his and I could feel him kissing my cheek." I see Connor stiffen out of the corner of my eye. "Then everything went pure brilliant white. I don't know how long for, but it felt amazing. I could have stayed there forever. I just gradually floated back, kind of like a feather floating back to earth and then you were sitting beside me in the cave. Does that make sense?"

"Perfect sense. You have had an amazing experience, Lucy. One that I, and those in the Priesthood train for a very long time to accomplish. You have experienced a rebirth, but to be conscious of it is quite amazing. You let go of the old, you went back to the creator and received a beautiful healing and then you were reborn, most assuredly with more of yourself than you started with. You couldn't have picked a better time for a transformation." She beams at me. Connor is looking at me with awe from under his lashes.

"What do you mean?"

"Transformation. That's what the butterfly festival is all about. The caterpillar eats its own weight in food," she points at the hampers, "spins its cocoon around itself and goes inside," she points to the cave, "then comes out as a butterfly. How does it feel to be a butterfly?"

"Lighter. I feel lighter. Like everything I no longer need or everything that was holding me back has gone. It feels good. Really good."

"Excellent!" grins Imogen. "I really have to go. The Butterfly Festival opens tonight and there is still lots needing done." I make to rise. "No, stay here and have breakfast. It's important that you rest and take good care of yourself today. Transformation is hard work. Give your body time to integrate the changes. Connor, I'm counting on you to look after Lucy and make sure she takes it easy today."

"Of course, your Majesty."

"I'll see you both tonight." She hurries away.

I sit and eat the greens that Connor has given me. We avoid looking at each other. He pokes the fire and I stare at the water.

"I think I'll go for a swim."

He stands as I do. "Not too far. I don't want you to tire yourself out," he says quietly, unsure of himself.

"I just need to wash the last few days away. I won't be long."

I sink into the water. The icy cold invigorates me. I finally feel awake. I watch Connor pack everything away, keeping his back to me.

We walk back down the hill at a pace that would have a ninety year old falling asleep. We are tense with each other and say little. I'm surprised how tired I feel after three days of being comatose. My legs aren't as solid as I would like for careening down a steep hill. Maybe it's just as well we are going so slowly.

Just when I can't bear the tension anymore, I step on a submerged rock. I go over on my ankle and my knees give out when I try to rectify my posture. Connor tries to break my fall and topples landing on top of me. Not breathing, we stare at each other. Until we decide to move at the same time. We tussle and I end up on top of him. *Can this day get any more embarrassing?*

I heave myself off him and sit up. Mortified, I hide my face and I focus on my ankle. Connor crouches down beside me and takes my ankle in his hands.

"It's not broken." He looks up at me, flushed and disheveled. "Can you stand?"

"I'll try."

Connor stands and takes me under the shoulder to help

me up. Tentatively I put weight on my foot. I take a few steps and hobble around for a bit. It's hard to think with him holding on to me. It's hard not to lean closer.

"Do you think you can walk back?" He eyes me with concern.

"Yes, it's fine. A bit stiff but it will be OK in a few minutes."

We both look down as I try walking normally. He stops and pulls me to face him.

"Connor, I—."

"Lucy, I'm—."

We laugh nervously.

I inhale a shaky breath. "Connor, you were right—."

"No, Lucy, I wasn't."

"But you were! I realize how ungrateful I've been for everything in my life. I came here and everyone's been really generous and kind and helpful. And so have you. Especially you. I am really, really grateful to you. For everything." I stop to gulp more air. "I was too scared to even try. I'm sorry," I mumble, looking down at my feet.

"I'm the one that's sorry." My head jerks up. Sincerity shines in his eyes. "I shouldn't have said what I did. I didn't mean any of it, Lucy. Not really. I was tired. I had been on duty for days. I know it's no excuse but I have a lot of responsibility. All the folks descending on us from the other lands need to be kept safe. Lucien chewed me out for losing you after our argument and threatened to demote me."

"I'm really sorry, Connor."

"And I was frustrated with you. You have all this talent— I would love to be as gifted as you."

I'm about to return the compliment. I've never met anyone as talented as Connor – even in the Flowerlands. But as I contemplate his qualities – his exceptional craftsmanship, his ability to bring calm with a gentle word or a joke – I tune in to what he is saying.

"Imogen spoke to me and explained..."

"Explained what?"

"How hard all the work you are doing is, mirror work and the rest. How frightening we must seem to you. Oh yeah and I know what it's like to be frightened now, I'm not that perfect.

"I came to apologize and there was no sign of you. You scared me. There were only the hampers on the beach. I thought you'd gone swimming and drowned. I was running around like a maniac looking for clues. Eventually saw paw prints leading to the cave. There you were, oblivious. I wanted to kill you for scaring me so much."

"I'd say we're even then, wouldn't you?" I grin.

"Maybe we should kiss and make up?"

I freeze and stare at him petrified until he holds his hand out to me and we shake. *Why couldn't I just laugh and playfully kiss his cheek?*

CHAPTER SEVENTEEN

Their Majesties have turned up dressed to impress, draped in the finest silks laden with semi-precious stones that sparkle and blind. I have been placed at the top table next to Lucien. His superior presence and impeccable table manners make me nervous enough to drop my cutlery several times and knock over a glass of strawberry and elderflower wine. Unfortunately, not all over him but at his feet. When I realize I am directly in front of the Protectors' table, most notably the dark-haired, blue-eyed, demi-God, it feels less of a punishment. Connor even deigns to grace me with a half-smile when our eyes meet. In his dress uniform of silver and black silk, he is even more delicious than normal.

The Kings Garth and Andrew make long and tedious speeches, trying to out do each other and Imogen gives a thankfully short blessing. Fiona gives a speech that gets tawdrier the more she is egged on by the drunken revelers at the back. Even Lucien's face is flaming by the end. Finally, we are served our food. Not stew for once. Tonight our repast is fit for royalty, starting with a sea bass on a bed of toasted seaweed with a fennel dressing. Spice rubbed roast pork, a delicate salad of summer leaves and edible flowers drizzled with marigold and cumin for mains. A sensuous geranium and rose flavored torte to finish.

As the last plate is scraped and in some cases licked clean, the band strikes up sedately. The Royals get up to dance a formal waltz, but as folk gradually join the floor the band descend into jigs and reels and rigidity is shirked off as everyone begins to enthusiastically fly around the floor.

I melt into the background and descend into the shadows as soon as I can. I turn and make my way carefully back to the castle.

"Hey Lucy, wait up." I turn to find Connor sprinting toward me. "Where are you going? The party is just starting. I was hoping for a dance." He's smiling and relaxed. I'm surprised to find tears prickling. "Are you OK?" His smile drops away and a frown mars his face.

"I'm really tired." Tears start running down my cheeks. "It's too loud. Too many people. I'm too raw." He steps closer and wipes my tears with his fingers.

"You're bound to be sensitive after the last few days," he says, coming to hug me. To my horror, I begin to sob into his chest. "Dance with me," he whispers when my sobs subside. I rest my head on his shoulder, my trunk hangs down his back as he starts to gently sway.

The moon comes out from behind a cloud and we are bathed in a silver shimmering light. Stars are strung across the indigo sky. I could stay here forever. His arms around me. His chin resting on my head and my body snuggled into him so all I can hear is the pounding of our hearts. He eventually takes a step back and looks down at me.

"Our first dance. Wasn't so bad, was it?"

We walk back to the castle through the illuminated forest. With a hasty kiss on the cheek, Connor says goodnight. He watches me thoughtfully until I close the heavy door.

Not so many hours later, I am rudely shaken awake by an exuberant and rather child-like Protector.

"Connor!"

"The day's half gone."

It can't be more than five o'clock. I pull my comforter over my head.

"Come on, I have a surprise for you."

I groan and roll myself up to sitting, flicking back the curtains. He's right; the day is half gone. The sun blazes high in the sky. He grabs me by the paw and pulls me outside.

I screech to a halt when we reach the clearing. Folk are swarming everywhere. There is every creature known and unknown to man, from huge trolls that cause the ground to vibrate when they walk to delicate floating flower faeries. The jubilant noises are chaotic, the color dazzlingly brilliant. I get an instant rush of excitement as the buzz of anticipation hits me.

Connor and I walk through the lines. He's barely patient with me as I ooh and ah over every little thing. There are stalls full of jewelry, sculpture, trinkets, clothing, jams, baking, meats, candles, hardware, homeware, antiques. Everything from the practical to the opulent to the whimsical to the beautiful. Beside me, Connor is acting like a five year old on Christmas Eve.

I see why when he pulls me in front of an easel with a large canvas facing the summer meadows. There is a wooden crate filled with jars, brushes tucked in a corner. I try pulling my trunk from his grasp but he doesn't let go.

"I know you're scared, Lucy," his voice soft and soothing. "Action is the key to all success. You cannot succeed if you don't even try. Ask yourself is it your light or your dark that you are afraid of?"

"Come again?" I frown.

"Are you scared that you'll fail or are you procrastinating because your terrified you'll succeed?" My stomach cramps. "Shine your light, Lucy. It's an insult to the creator to hide. Let the world see your brilliance. It's time," he says softly.

He gives my trunk one last stroke and releases it. I step to the easel and sit myself down. I pick up a brush and a jar of paint. I dab some grass green paint onto my brush and stare accusingly at the canvas and the meadows in front of it. I fidget and stare some more and some more. I sigh, frustrated with myself.

Connor unfolds a stool and sits behind me. His legs slide around me, his front nearly at my back.

"Don't think about it. Thinking is the destroyer of all creativity." His breath tickles the shell of my ear.

I turn my head to look at him over my shoulder. "Do you paint?"

He shakes his head. "Metal and glass are my mediums." *Profound, hot and creative.* "Don't use what's in here," he taps my forehead. "Use what's in here," he places his hand over my rapidly beating heart, "and here," he places his other hand over my tummy, his lips nearly touching mine. I swallow and turn back to the easel. I'm no longer thinking, just tingling.

When I look up again, the sun is low in the sky. Only a few stragglers near the meadows. Connor is lying in the grass beside me, asleep. I have the beginnings of a great picture. I have sketched the outline of the distant hills. Added the first coat on the brilliant blue sky with a lone wispy cloud that resembles a rising phoenix. I am really pleased that I have managed to catch the color and diversity of the meadow flowers. I've painted the cool blue lavender, the warm orange-red of wild poppies, smaller than what I'm used to seeing. The aloofness of the white yarrow standing to attention. Outlandish pink coneflowers dancing to get noticed. The vibrant yellow of the black-eyed Susan, their black centers a perfect foil to their sunny yellow petals. The dandelion seeds floating lazily by on the breeze.

I stand and stretch as I inspect my handiwork. I can see myself trailing through the meadow dressed as a nineteenth century lady. Long flowing white dress and wide brimmed beribboned hat to keep me pure. The plants swaying gently as my skirts brush them on the way past. My fingers trailing over petals. I can smell the cool calming fragrance of the lavender drifting up as I crush some fallen flower heads beneath my unladylike bare feet. The long grass rustles in the gentle summer breeze. I stop and lift my face to the

111

blazing sun, risking freckles. I feel the burn against my palm as I pull a head of grass through my hand, letting the seeds fall from my splayed fingers to find new life in the meadow. I see myself bending down to talk to one of the flower faeries.

The faeries are next on my agenda for painting. I've not quite figured out how to paint the different personalities they take from their flowers. The wild nature of the poppy faerie, fiery like their flowers, wearing the ruffled dresses and shirts of the flamenco dancer, black wings emerging. The calming coolness of the lavender faerie keeps the poppy faerie from spontaneously combusting with Latin passion. I'll paint the cool greys and lilacs of their clothing and wings.

The pure white of the yarrow who does her best to remain detached from her contemporaries, sitting in white Grecian robes, arms and white gossamer wings wrapped round her knees keeping the world at bay, or him standing erect and untouchable, like marble. The look-at-me cocking and preening of the bright pink cone faerie. Bubble-pink dress or trousers and sparkling metallic wings with a giggling and delighted nature. The laid back, chillax-dude, there's no rush nature of the black-eyed Susan faeries that remind me of surfing or sunbathing on a hot summers day.

Connor carries all my supplies back to my studio. I carry my treasure carefully back to my bedroom where I hang it to dry.

"Not bad, not bad at all." I hug myself.

CHAPTER EIGHTEEN

The penultimate day of the festival, midsummer's eve, is when the butterflies break free of their cocoons.

When I arrive at the summer meadows early, the clearing is already full. I soon learn that folks have been here since first light trying to get the best position to view the spectacle. Connor stands as I arrive and silently beckons me over to a rug at the very front. I clamber over to him, bumping heads and bodies and wings here and there, even managing to squish a few toes.

"Aren't you working today?" I ask Connor, who is sitting slouched on the rug, more relaxed than I've ever known him.

"Nobody works until the butterflies stop dancing, not even the Protectors."

I have an amazing view of the meadows. The flowers are tall and in full bloom. They are a riot of color: pink, white, yellow, orange, purple, red and blues, wild and free. The air is still. Folks are silent. Even the birds are holding their chatter.

The butterflies begin breaking through each chrysalis at almost the same time, a move that is random although seemingly orchestrated. Tentatively they flutter their wings, getting acquainted with their new form and then the whispering breeze slowly and gently carries the butterflies into the air. Thousands upon thousands of the colorful winged creatures take to the skies and dance. They swirl and sweep, loop and lunge, land and take off from flowers in formation, in chaos and then in order. The display runs contrary to all the Laws of Nature. It is afternoon before the butterflies settle onto the flowers to take a well-earned rest.

"What now?" I ask.

"Now the fun really begins."

"What do you mean?" A dais has been erected in the summer meadows just beyond the crowd. Six chairs are being placed upon the platform.

"The Marriage Forum," says Connor, hugging his knees. "The Kings and Queens and priest and priestess decide who is to get married. The couples will approach all four of them with their families. If the families give the go-ahead, Brother Michael and Sister Sapphire analyze their aura to ensure they are compatible, then the kings and queens vote yay or nay."

I pull a face. It all sounds a bit harsh.

"How a couple are together affects the whole community. This way, the whole community gets to decide."

"But you said it's only the people on stage that decide."

"Oh no. Any one of us can stand up and object at any time until the final decision is made."

"A festival and forum are held once a year in each of the lands. Spring in Fiona's lands in the East. Summer here obviously, autumn in Garth's lands in the West and winter in Andrew's lands in the North. Most folks want to get married in the summer, so this is the most popular forum."

"There's quite a lot of interest," I say, staring at the queue that has formed.

There must be about thirty couples. Ranging from the young to the very old. There is a very young couple in front of the podium. They are both faeries, they have that really cheesy couple thing going on and have dressed in matching salmon pink outfits. Even their wings match and stretch to stay touching; they can't take eyes or hands off each other. I am stunned when I see Imogen smile and everyone on the podium nods at the same time. A cheer goes up from a nearby group who then surrounds them.

"No way," I say, shocked. "I can't believe they said yes. I mean, they must be my age!"

"Have you got something against marriage, Lucy?"

"No, but they are so young."

"And yet so ready."

Next there is a really old decrepit elfish couple with sticks to help them walk. I turn and look at Connor questioningly. He is lying casually on his side, head leaning on his elbow, clearly amused by me. I'm too fascinated to wonder why his eyes never leave my face.

"That's Sam and Mary. They like to renew their vows every year. They've done this for the last two hundred." *Oh* I mouth silently and turn back to the queue.

Next there is a troll couple dressed in slate grey shirts and trousers with pink and purple tufts on their heads. They both look like they are made out of granite. Then there is a hobbit couple both dressed in dark green tunics with bird's nests in their hair. A pixie couple next; one with beige skin, her partner with olive skin both with long dark brown hair dressed in forest green khaki shirts and trousers and no shoes.

The next couple causes some consternation in the crowd and a lot of discussion amongst the Royalty. There is an elfish man, tall with ash blond hair and pale white skin and blue eyes, and he is dressed brown shirt, three quarter length trousers and tan suede ankle boots. He has a leather strap crisscrossed across his chest and a bow and arrows strapped to his back. Next to him is the most beautiful, sensual and mesmerizing woman I've ever come across. She has bronze hair, olive skin and moss-green eyes. She is dressed in a filmy brown and green thin-strapped gown to her ankles that caresses her as she sways forward. I can't take my eyes off her. There is a lot of deliberating. Finally the Kings and Queens shake their heads.

"What's going on?" I ask Connor.

He flicks his eyes from me to the stage. "That's Hermann, the hunter and Giselle. Lovely isn't she?"

I bristle at his words. "I don't know. She's perfectly ordinary," I sniff.

Connor barks out a laugh. "You're cute when you are jealous."

"I'm not jealous!"

"You should be." I stare dumbfounded. *What does he mean?* "She's a wood nymph. It's her job to entice men into the woods and have her way with them."

"What?" I say, horrified. "Have you..." My face heats and I have to look away.

"Don't worry, Lucy. I'm trained to resist," he whispers gruffly. "Lucien insists upon it." He frowns. "We spent too much of our time breaking up arguments between spouses and partners and fae-men and women that had been lured into the woods. The nymphs are free spirits. Their job is to entertain as many men or women as possible."

"There are male nymphs?" My eyes light up.

"Not for you." Connor scowls. I beam. Jealousy's a sexy look on him. He looks back at the stage. "Nymphs are not meant to be in relationships. It's in their nature to be flighty. That's why their petition has been denied."

"That's not fair! What if she's not like that? What if she's different from the other nymphs? I mean, she's here asking to commit to one person."

"That's why they have been asked to wait a year. They weren't told no."

"How do you know all that?"

"I can lip read," he says, eyeing my lips.

"I'll bear that in mind." I turn back to queue.

There are a few more faerie couples, a few elfish couples, a troll and one of those fierce wee hairy things and a hobbit and a pixie.

Connor leaves me to continue ogling and gets us some hot food from one of the sellers. I thank Connor and take the warm chicken and salad stuffed pitta-bread from him as he sits. Dylan grabs the other.

"Hey!" says Connor as Dylan grins and bites.

"Never leave out your brothers," mumbles Dylan with his mouth full.

"Here, have mine," I say, handing over the sandwich.

"We'll share." He takes a bite and holds the pitta out to me to bite. It is far too intimate. My tummy begins to leap, especially with him looking at me so intensely.

"Only two more fools to go," mutters Dylan. "It's ridiculous. I mean, who wants to get married?" he says taking the last bite, interrupting our staring.

"Imogen," I say.

Dylan chokes on his food.

"Imogen is getting married. In a few moments she is announcing her betrothal," I say gently.

"And you know that how?" demands Dylan.

"Fiona told me. The Commander asked her to marry him yesterday and she has said yes."

"But she can't," wails Dylan. "She's supposed to marry me!"

CHAPTER NINETEEN

King Garth has stood up. "Ladies and gentlemen."

"Why didn't you ask her then?" I hiss. Everyone round about turns on me and tells me to *shush*.

"There was never a right time," he groans, flinging his arm over his eyes. "Now it's too late."

"I have special announcement for you today..."

"It's never too late, Dylan," I say.

Shush is hissed at us from every direction.

"It is my great pleasure to announce the betrothal of Queen Imogen and..." An *oh* and then an *ah* loud enough for Garth to pause goes up from all the folks around us listening to our conversation.

"—Commander Lucien of the Queen's Protectors."

A huge roar goes up from the crowd as Lucien takes Imogen's hand.

I jump to my feet and a huge trumpeting reverberates around the meadows, ricocheting off the distant hills and scaring the twittering birds from their perches. My trunk! I have sounded my trunk and will not be silenced.

"I object," I call clearly.

To my surprise, Connor stands up besides me. "I object," he yells towards the stage. He looks angry.

119

After a long silence,

"What are your objections, Lucy?" calls Andrew.

"I believe it is in the interest of the whole community to allow the *other* interested party a chance to declare himself. That party would like to do so now. Come on, Dylan," I hiss out of the corner of my mouth. "It's now or never." I wrap my trunk round his arm and pull.

Dylan stumbles to his feet.

"Come forward," commands Garth.

Dylan staggers towards to the dais in a trance. His trembling legs carry him in front of a stunned Imogen. He lowers shakily to his knees and takes the hand Lucien isn't holding in his.

"Imogen," he croaks, clearing his throat he begins again. "Imogen…" He gulps in a breath, blowing it out slowly.

"I love you." His declaration rings out across the clearing. He locks eyes with Imogen. "I love everything about you, your smile, the way your eyes light up when you are happy, the way they turn deep purple when you are angry. I love your generous spirit and your enormous heart." He exhales in a rush. "I guess what I'm trying to say is forgive me please, for many things, but most especially for not doing this sooner. I didn't want to ask because I didn't want you stuck with me if I found myself in darkness again."

"That's why you didn't propose?" Imogen looks at him incredulously. "You of all people should know that my love isn't conditional."

"I know it *now*. So will you make me the happiest faerie alive and become my wife?" Imogen's tears spill over as she nods.

Dylan whoops and jumps up, grabs Imogen under the knees, lifts her and spins her around. The crowd is in an uproar. A few fiddles are being screeched awake ready to celebrate.

"Just a minute," calls an old man with a long white beard and faded blue robes. "The Queen has accepted two proposals of marriage. The ancient rules state that in the case of two suitors there must be a fight to the death." The crowd gasps.

"There'll be no fights to the death," says Lucien firmly.

"But Commander," splutters the old man. "Rule eight hundred and twenty three states…"

"I don't care about your rules," roars Lucien.

"The rules state…" whimpers the old man.

"There is an easy way to sort this out," says Queen Fiona. "Dylan and Lucien will have a contest."

"Whoever wins gets to marry Queen Imogen," says King Garth.

CHAPTER TWENTY

Surrounded by Protectors, Lucien looks menacing in a black sleeveless tunic and martial art style trousers. The tribal tattoo curling round his upper arm dances as his biceps bulge. His solid arm and thigh muscles ripple when he gracefully parries to and fro with his sparring partner.

Dylan's sinuous and rather elegant body looks inadequate in comparison. He is waving his rapier about amateurishly, joking with the crowd, asking for pointers on how to use it.

"Oh God," I groan. Dylan takes five steps back. Lucien does the same and takes his rapier from his second.

"Pass Dylan his rapier," whispers Connor, nudging me forward. I have no idea why Dylan chose me to second him.

"Thanks," Dylan grins and winks as he takes the rapier from my shaking hands.

On the drop of a white hanky the two men bend their knees, point fences and lunge at each other. The clash of steel rings out as the blades scratch against each other. Parry, parry, and lunge.

Dylan stumbles, falling flat on his face as Lucien is declared the winner.

The men are allowed time to refuel and recover some energy before the next event begins. Dylan comes over and gulps down a pitcher of water.

"Only two points in it." He grins and flops back into the grass.

The crowd is buoyant as we all make our way into the forest for the tree climb, stopping beside an ancient pine tree. The crowd fans out in a circle. Dylan takes off his boots and socks and hands them to me before rolling his trousers up, barefoot in a bed of pine needles. They are to climb at different sides of the same huge pine tree.

"On your marks. Go," calls the referee.

Lucien takes off up the tree. Dylan stands casually at the bottom looking up. Lucien is already ten feet in the air.

"Will you hurry?" I yell at him.

He places his first foot on the bark. He turns to me and grins. Bounces on one foot, once, twice, thrice and he's off. Climbing like a demented monkey. Lucien has spied his rapid progress and is scrambling so hard to get higher that his foot slips. The whole crowd cries out. He manages to grab a branch at the last minute, saving himself from a hundred-foot fall. He swings to get his leg up on the branch. He misses. His fingers start slipping. We all gasp. I grip Connor's hand. No one has been paying attention to Dylan, who has maneuvered his way to Lucien. He sits with his leg dangling either side of the solid limb, reaches out for Lucien's free hand and heaves.

"Ready?" Lucien nods at him.

Dylan scrambles his way back to the other side whilst Lucien gets himself up to standing. Then Dylan climbs so fast he is almost a blur. Grabs the red flag and is declared the winner. I scream and cover my eyes as he throws himself off the tree. There is no thud of a crashing body. I open my eyes to find a grinning Dylan right in front of me, still flapping his wings.

When we reach the river, the kayaks are already in the water. Most folk are waiting at the finish line a mile downstream. Although the water is running fast, the level is low. Rocks are jutting out everywhere waiting to ground a rower or smash a hull or a skull.

They are waiting for me. I wade into the water up to my chest and hold the tail of Dylan's kayak with my trunk whilst he jumps in. Lucien's second has his back. With a one, two, three we push them off. I drag myself through the water to the riverbank, where Connor is waiting to help me out.

We race through the trees trying to keep abreast of the action. I catch glimpses of the two men rushing towards rocks and narrowly missing huge boulders and each other. Dylan is just in front of Lucien. Low water levels mean they have to follow the same tight channels, making it impossible to overtake. Dylan leads the whole way. Amazingly, we make it to the finish before the racers. Connor, Lucien's second and I are all red and panting. We elbow our way to the front of the crowd to catch the boats and watch as

Lucien slows and floats towards us, ramming his paddle into the water.

"Where's Dylan?" yells Imogen over the cheers.

CHAPTER TWENTY-ONE

An overturned kayak floats towards us. Lucien paddles to the middle of the river to create a barricade. I stand rigid as Queen Fiona dives headfirst into the water. A brilliant metallic green fish tail rises above the water then disappears. One elephant, two elephants, three, four… ten…twenty elephants.

Still no Dylan. Still no Fiona.

Lucien is paddling furiously to stay still. I see the ripples as Fiona's head surfaces and she begins to swim for shore, biceps bulging as she pulls an unconscious Dylan with her. Connor and three Protectors reach the bank and splash into the river. They grab Dylan from Fiona and haul him out of the water. Dylan's lips are blue. Blood steaks down his face from a nasty gash on his forehead. I sag against Connor with relief as Dylan finally coughs and spews out river water.

Someone has handed Imogen a first-aid kit. She pours white fluid onto gauze. Dylan hisses as she puts the pad on his forehead. The smell of neat alcohol wafts towards me.

"Did I win?" grimaces Dylan as Imogen starts to sew up his cut.

"No," she says curtly.

"Oh well. I'll get him in the next round," he says, closing his eyes.

"There won't be a next round," says Imogen. "You aren't fit to continue. I'm declaring Lucien the winner."

"Imogen," says Lucien.

But Imogen and Dylan are locked in their own private battle.

"The hell you are," yells Dylan. "I'm fine." He gets unsteadily to his feet and looks around drunkenly.

"You are barely compos mentis."

"You want to marry Lucien?" says Dylan, his voice scaling several octaves.

"I won't have you kill yourself over this." The two of them glare at each other.

"Your Majesty?" Lucien tries again.

"What is it?" snaps Imogen.

"I request your permission to relinquish my proposal and withdraw from the competition."

"Hell no!" yells Dylan.

"I'll not have you kill yourself over this," says Lucien.

"If you win, I might as well die," yells Dylan. All color drains from Lucien's face. "And don't even consider letting me win."

He turns to Imogen. "I'm not withdrawing. He's..." he jerks a thumb over his shoulder, "not withdrawing. Live with it," he yells at Imogen.

"Fine. Kill yourself you stupid man. See if I care," yells Imogen. "You have one hour before the next event. Lucy, take him to Sister Sapphire."

She floats off regally.

*

"Oh my god, Dylan." I drop to my knees beside him.

"I'm fine Lucy," he slurs. "Just need a wee catnap. Then I'll be hunky dory. You'll see."

"Dylan?" I try shaking him. Nothing. No eyes opening. No grunts. Nothing.

"What should I do?" I say.

"Let's get him into the recovery position." Lucien crouches and easily maneuvers Dylan onto his stomach, head to the side, right arm and leg bent. "He'll be OK. He has miraculous powers of recovery." I raise my eyebrow. "We've had a fair few tussles. He's even beat me a time or two."

"Dylan beat you?" Huh!

"Oh good, you're here." Lucien stands as Connor approaches with Sister Sapphire.

She kneels down and touches Dylan. I'm not sure if I imagine the pink light being funneled out of Sister Sapphire's hands into Dylan. Finally, with a contented sigh Dylan rolls over, opens his eyes, stretches, turns his head and grins at us. Lucien holds out a hand and pulls him to his feet.

"Come on you little shit. Let's go get you a Queen."

Next is a climb up the side of a mountain and a sprint back down. This is Lucien's best event, and with the score two-one to Lucien, it's not looking good for Dylan. I watch as Dylan scrambles up the cliff face. He makes it to the top well ahead of Lucien and jogs down the hill, jigging a victory dance. A barely concealed snigger comes from the direction of the Protectors as Dylan gets down on bended knee in front of Imogen, lifts the back of her hand to his lips and kisses it.

"If you've changed your mind and want that big oaf over there, speak now or forever hold your peace."

"Get up and get on with it! I've waited long enough." Imogen yanks her hand out of Dylan's grip, crosses her arms and turns away from him hiding a smile. Dylan stands up with a flourish, bows and grins.

"It's a good job I love you so much or else you might end up married to that *eejit* Lucien."

"Careful Dylan," calls Lucien.

With that, the wind picks up and the earth is bathed in shadow. I look up to the underside of enormous wings. The creature, coming in to land, skims so close that I have to duck my head.

"What is it?" I ask Connor in awe.

"Dragon." I look up at him and he grins. "Racing dragons." I move towards Dylan. When I reach him he is gulping great lungful's of air.

"Breathe," I say, grabbing his shoulders. "Remember why you are doing this."

He looks at me with panicked eyes. "Why am I doing this again?"

"To make sure she doesn't end up married to me," says Lucien, sauntering over to his dragon.

We walk over to the dragon together. It is huge and cherry red with coal black eyes. I walk over slowly and hold out my hand. The creature breathes out a hot steamy breath and nudges me with its nose. I run my hand over its scales, smooth as glass, and the dragon purrs in ecstasy as my hand glides over its flanks.

Dylan takes a few steps and begins to run. He leaps up onto the dragon's wings and onto its back. Meanwhile, Lucien has mounted the back of a cerulean blue dragon and the dragons flap their wings and take off with a massive *whoosh*.

The dragons hover level until someone blows a whistle and they climb higher and higher until they are nearly in the clouds. Then they really take off. They dive and fly close to the ground before climbing quickly towards the mountains. They fly over the mountains and dive down the other side. When they come round a break in the hills, they are flying neck and neck.

They bank to make it through the gap in the mountains. Someone screams. I watch in horror as Lucien loses his grip and slips off the back of his dragon, falling at crushing speed towards the ground. Dylan looks back to check Lucien's position, reining in, he spins and turns. Sweeping low he manages to get under Lucien mere feet from the hard earth. When Dylan lands, Lucien is lying facing backwards on his stomach over the tail. Without its rider, Lucien's dragon has taken off for the great unknown. Lucien sits up and turns so that he is sitting with his chest to Dylan's back and they return sedately. The dragon comes in for a graceful landing, smoothly skimming the earth until it comes to a halt past the finish line.

CHAPTER TWENTY-TWO

"As both finished together, technically I should call the race is a draw," says Garth loud enough for the crowd to hear.

"But I won't," he grins.

The whole crowd comes forward to congratulate them. I get there first, kissing and hugging them both. I'm jostled out the way by a big grey walking boulder. "Excuse me" rumbles the troll. I'm shoved further back by a wispy pixie floating by, whose strength to weight ratio is ridiculous. A thick stump of oak or hobbit crawls through my legs. "Pardon Me," he says. On and on it goes: electric blue faerie with moss green wings, an elf with violet eyes and olive skin, a white gossamer nymph more sensuality than substance. Her male counterpart drifts by and my body zings, every nerve ending tingles, my neck tilts back exposing my throat as I take a long languorous breath, inhaling the intoxicatingly sweet chocolate scent of him. My body immediately tries to follow him but the crowd have closed ranks ejecting me from their midst.

Alone, on the outside again. I watch as the whole community gathers round, full of simple joy.

I turn and wander through the woods until the setting sun makes it difficult to navigate. I find a cooling rock to lie back on and watch as the first stars begin to twinkle. This isn't my life and if it is I don't know how long for. Will I get to see Dylan and Imogen's wedding? Their baby? Will Connor and I ever share a kiss? Will I ever see my parents again? My stomach lurches and I jolt to sitting. What if I never see Connor again?

"There you are," pants a hot and sweaty Connor. "I've been looking all over for you." He lets out a shrill whistle, which is echoed back from several directions.

I stare at him. Committing every beautiful part of him to memory. His eyes, hair, lips, his glistening body. Everything. His strength, his virility, his care, his kindness, his sheer magnetism. I absorb and absorb and absorb until Connor shifts uncomfortably. He holds his hand out to me.

"Come on, the party has started."

We amble back to the summer meadows. There are folk from all four lands celebrating. Dylan and Imogen are dancing together in the center of the dance floor, eyes only for each other. I reluctantly allow Connor to drag me up to dance. He steps in and pulls me close, like the night in the forest. I rest my head against his chest and he leans his head on mine as we slowly sway. A single perfect dance. If this is all I get, I'll take it.

CHAPTER TWENTY-THREE

When I awake my bedroom is a golden chamber of shimmering light. I raise my arms and stretch. It feels good to have every muscle in my body protest. Hours of dancing are a great workout. My bed is cozy and my room cavernous. I snuggle down and enjoy the comfort a while longer.

It's no use, I'm restless.

Eager to see everyone, I sit up and swing my legs over the side of my bed and put my feet on the floor. I look at my knees. Something isn't right but I'm not sure what. That something is keeping it to itself. *Oh well.* I get up. At least, I try to. What I actually do is fall on my face with a resounding *thud*. I press my hands into the floor and push myself to sitting and stretch my legs out in front of me. My face crinkles in confusion as I stare.

A tousled Dylan in only pajama bottoms comes rushing in. "Uh-oh," he says and turns away out of the door.

"Dylan?" I say, looking up at where he had been.

"Oh my," says Imogen, rushing in and coming to stand over me.

"What? What is it?" I still don't know what's wrong. I

feel panic taking over. There is a knock and my bedroom door opens and an arm curls round it, dangling a white shirt from the index finger.

"Here, put this on," says Imogen, handing the shirt to me. She pokes her head round the door.

"You can come in now. She's covered."

"Imogen?" Fear is making my voice tight. Without a word, Imogen and Dylan each place a hand under my elbow and heave me to standing. The shirt comes to my knees. Imogen and Dylan take me on unsteady legs out into the hall. Gasps come from the dozen or so faeries and Protectors gathered outside my door, making my legs even wobblier. Dylan and Imogen all but carry me to a room at the end of the hall. We walk in. There is an open flower shaped bed draped in indigo silk and velvet, matching brocade curtains, a silver chenille chaise longue. I look around and wonder why they have brought me here.

They stop in front of floor-to-ceiling mirror. I look. Then I look again. My eyes widen with realization.

"Oh my God," I pant. My fingers gently caress my skin. I move my head and peer into the mirror and start pulling and prodding my face.

"It's me," I say breathlessly. "It's me!" I turn back to the mirror in wonder. I am so happy to see my face again. My blue eyes. My cute nose. My pink lips. I raise my hand and run my fingers through my long wavy blond hair. I raise my hands in front of my face. Four fingers and a thumb and soft, soft skin. Nails! I open and close my hands, make fists and release them. My eyes travel down to my knees. No wrinkles. Down my calves, which are positively svelte compared to elephant legs, to slender ankles. I splay my toes.

"What does it mean?" I gush, turning to Imogen. "Am I going home?" My stomach knots with anticipation.

"Not yet," says Imogen softly. "We still have some work to do."

"But why have I been turned human again if I'm not going home?"

"I don't know, Lucy. I don't have all the answers. Dylan, can you fetch Tatiana and ask her to speak to the cobbler?"

"Tatiana?" I squeak. Imogen all seeing eyes bore into me.

"Problem?" asks Imogen. My head shakes before my voice can answer.

News travels quickly, and Imogen shoos everyone away as she instructs a Protector to bring me breakfast.

"Are you feeling OK?" asks Imogen as I lay back on her chaise-longue.

"I'm sore all over and tired but wired. You know?"

"Metamorphosis takes a lot out of you. Be gentle with yourself today, OK?" I nod and pull the velvet throw over me while I wait.

I surface to Tatiana frowning above me, barely concealing her disdain. I feel myself bristle. She *wheechs* the throw off me. "Come on, up with you." I pull the shirt down over my knees, scoot out the bed and stand with my arms around my waist.

"That'll never do," she says. "Off with it." She points to the shirt. My eyes widen in horror.

"I need to measure you. I also want to see your body shape and your skin tone to see what will suit you best."

Her foot starts tapping. I unbutton the shirt, slowly slide it off and lay it on the bed. Tatiana whips out a measuring tape and a little wooden book and pencil. She tuts as she moves my hands from my breasts and uncrosses my legs. She raises my arms up and out and begins taking measurements. I may as well be a mannequin.

"I'll just go make your clothes." She scarpers out the door. I only just make out Imogen saying "I trust you to be professional Tatiana," and a flustered "of course Majesty," that makes me smile.

I mindlessly pop autumn berries and nuts into my mouth, ignoring the vibrant reds and purples of the berries or their succulent flavors as they burst on my tongue and trickle down my throat or the sweet creamy texture of the hazelnuts as I chew.

I have just finished my fennel and blackberry tea when Tatiana returns. She lays out several sets of underwear. All silk with lace edging. I pick out a lavender bra and pants combination edged with fuchsia pink lace. I step into them. They fit perfectly. Tatiana holds out a bluebell colored dress. I raise my arms above my head. Tatiana floats up and lifts the dress over me. It glides down my body in one fluid movement.

It has a tactile silk slip lining with chiffon over-layers and long floaty sleeves. The hem is a couple of inches above my knees, much shorter than anything I would normally wear.

She holds out a pair of bluebell colored, flower embroidered ballet pumps and a pair of gray lace-up ankle boots. Today I go for the shoes.

Tatiana frowns briefly. "I need to take in the waist." She turns my back to her so that I'm facing the mirror.

"How long have you been in love with Connor?" Tatiana's head jerks up and her eyes widen. I suck in a breath in surprise both from the words that have just left my mouth and the pin now embedded in my flesh.

"How did you know?" She fiddles with the dress.

"The way you looked at him when you were dancing."

"Oh." She stands taking my dress off at the same time. She sits on the chaise, picks up a needle and thread and begins to sew.

"Look," I turn away from the mirror, "I'm sorry I didn't realize Connor was already taken."

"He's not." She finally looks at me, her eyes damp with threatening tears. "The feeling isn't mutual." I'm annoyed at my sudden need to comfort her.

"I was lonely when I first arrived. Far away from home. Someone shows me a bit of kindness and in my desperate state maybe I misread the signals or something?"

"You didn't. Everyone knows he's totally besotted with you."

"He is?" My belly suddenly fills with butterflies. *It's real?*

"Well, yeah. How can you not know? He gave you his mother's brushes and remodeled her studio for you *before* you got here."

"He did?" I quickly hide my glee when I see the desolation on her face.

"He hasn't been out with a girl in two years. It's not for the lack of offers. We all thought he was going to come out." I stare incredulously at her.

"He's not that kind of faerie," I say, scowling as I cross my arms across my chest.

"It's not that far fetched, look at those eyelashes and the face, not to mention his body." She stares off into the distance. I glower at her, resisting the urge to shout MINE!

"I've made you tights for the winter. We'll get a cloak organized for the weather turning. Hair." She goes behind me and begins to tug and pull. "There." She spins me back to the mirror.

I look at my face. I've missed it. My hair has been pinned into goddess braids with some trailing strands making it look effortless. I've got cheekbones!

I swish this way and that. I look good in the dress, really good. My blue-grey eyes look lavender. My skin is glowing; its paleness a perfect contrast to the bluebell shade, the porcelain perfection of a Victorian beauty. My figure is amazing; it resembles that of a 1950s pin-up girl. I try a Marilyn pose. I'm amazed, I don't look ridiculous. I look… well, hot.

"It's the most beautiful dress I've ever seen. Thank you."

I turn and startle Tatiana with a hug.

CHAPTER TWENTY-FOUR

The clink of steel blades reaches me as I skip out of the faerie castle and head towards the noise. Passers by are protected from the combatants by a wooden board skirting the outer edge of the forecourt. I realize it's needed when one protector thumps against it, startling me. My eyes are so busy scanning for Connor that it takes me a few moments to notice silence descending.

When I look around everyone on the training ground has turned in my direction. Some have their swords raised, resting against the sword opposite, only their heads turned towards me. Others have dropped their arms and the sword tip is resting in the earth. Some Protectors are standing to attention, others leaning casually on their weapons, but they are all staring. Color washes over my cheeks until I can feel them burning.

It's Lucien who breaks the spell as he strolls casually up to me.

"Good Morning, Lucy. Did the butterflies inspire you the other day?"

"Hmm, maybe." I duck my head.

Lucien bends very close and whispers in my ear,

"He's in the back right-hand corner." It's then that I notice Connor. Fists clenched. A black tension gripping his features. "Break-time gentlemen," Lucien calls, then leans down to me. "You haven't seen Dylan have you? He's been AWOL all morning."

"I...um... think Imogen has him tied up." Lucien guffaws then strides away.

The men lean their weapons against the barricades and make for the tea table. I stand looking at Connor, who is staring at me. I am struck with indecision. Should I stay or should I go and let Connor have his tea? He is sweaty and hot as are all the men. The morning must have been a hard workout. Lucien's payback for yesterday? The decision is made for me when Connor saunters towards me with focused intent. I watch as he puts his hand on the barricade and swings his legs easily over to land in front of me.

"Hi," he says softly.

My cheeks burn when I look up and see he is staring at me.

"You look beautiful. I mean, you were beautiful before. But this..." His voice catches and he runs agitated fingers through his hair. "I've never met anyone as beautiful as you."

My jaw drops. I don't know what to say. I feel beautiful when I'm with him. I look beyond Connor. His colleagues are spread out on raised benches across from us. It is an incongruous sight, these warriors sitting gracefully sipping tea from china cups and saucers, watching us as if we are in a play. I look back at him.

"There you are," calls Dylan, racing up to us. "Sorry, am I interrupting?" he says in all innocence.

"You have a talent for it," says Connor through gritted teeth.

"Lucy and I have a date," grins Dylan. He puts his arm round my shoulder and begins to walk us away, but Connor grabs my hand and pulls me back to him.

"Go out with me tonight?" My hand tingles from his touch. My lips twitch into a delighted smile as I nod.

Cheering and whistling erupts from our audience. A grinning Connor leaps the barricade and saunters to the tea urn.

CHAPTER TWENTY-FIVE

I drop my nose and inhale the sweet scent of wild flowers.

"These are lovely, Connor." He flashes a dimple at me. "Ready?"

I nod and grab my cloak. Connor takes my hand and begins to run.

"What's the hurry? Slow down," I laugh. We've been running for ages. I'm surprised I can still talk.

"Sorry, I'm excited." He grins sheepishly. I give a soppy grin in return. He has stopped running but we are still walking at a snapping pace.

"Connor, please," I say, tugging his hand.

"Please you I shall, fair maiden." Without releasing my hand he stops and drops into a courtly bow.

"Where are we going anyway?"

"Patience. It's a surprise." He kisses the tip of my nose then loops his arm over my shoulders. I loop mine round his waist and we hurry on.

Connor steps behind me and covers my eyes just when I begin to glimpse a field in the distance. After too many unnerving steps over uneven ground unable to see, Connor lifts his hands away. "Ta da."

There in the center of the field is the most magnificent electric blue dragon with cherry red ridges and wings.

"Ready to go dragon riding?"

"On my own?"

"No, this is a two-man dragon. It takes years of training to ride solo." He takes my hand and places it where his had been, stroking the dragon's snout. It huffs warmth onto my hand. I bend and kiss the dragon's nose and continue to pet it whilst Connor talks technical with the dragon rider: wind speeds, air currents; all gibberish to me. I tune out and sweet-talk the dragon in ridiculous baby talk.

"He likes you," says Connor, hoisting himself onto the dragon's wing.

He holds out his hand to me and helps me clamber up. I lift my leg inelegantly over the dragon's back, slip and slide a bit and then manage to sit up and wrap my cloak tightly around myself. Connor leaps gracefully up and sits behind me, gripping me tightly with his hard thigh muscles. The dragon rider comes over and hands me a hot water bottle.

"It'll keep you warm up there."

My face flushes as the warmth spreads over my body.

"Don't you get one?" I turn my head to look at Connor.

"I don't need it." He pulls me hard against him. My back to his front. His head comes over my shoulder. "You get the best view, but that means you're the windbreak."

The dragon rider hands the reins to Connor, nods and steps out the way. Connor loops his arms under mine and holds the reins in his hands tight against my waist. He must feel me trembling.

"Don't worry. I've got you." I feel his thighs muscles contract as he grips me tighter. "And I'm not letting you go."

My spine tingles and my stomach dances as he whispers against my ear. I don't think he's talking about the dragon ride.

Connor clicks a command. A few powerful beats of the dragon's wings and we are airborne. Soaring over the Flowerlands, the summer meadows with its fading flowers. Over the forest where Connor points out the castle and the forge. I can see the barracks and the Protectors training. The village as everyone goes about their evening. We climb a little higher and fly over the Emerald Loch, the low evening sun reflecting on the glassy surface. A lone deer lifts its head as we fly over. We veer left, the dragon gains speed. We dip down over sandy beaches hugging the coastal seas. A mermaid waves at us from a rock as Connor points out different landmarks of Queen Fiona's lands.

He continues his commentary as we veer right flying over King Andrew's mountainous lands. He points to the many peaks giving me names I'll never remember of hills I'll never recognize, some green, some with russet bracken-covered sides. The valleys in between containing small villages, where smoke curls from chimneys as the heat of the day fades. Children run out of houses to wave to us as we glide past. Connor tells me when we are over King Garth's quilted lands, great patches of different colored greens divided by hedges and stone walls. We bank and circle round.

A grin is frozen on my numb face as we come in for a glacial landing. There's no bump as the dragon's feet land softly on terra firma. Its dragon rider comes rushing out of the trees and harnesses the beast. I lay my head back on Connor's shoulder and breathe in deeply, wallowing in him. I breathe in the exhilaration, letting it suffuse every single cell of my body. I want to be able to reach in and take the feeling of total freedom out whenever I need reminding.

"OK?" I turn my head to Connor and nod, allowing my grin to spread over my thawing face.

He bends his head, lips nearly touching mine.

"Sorry, Connor. I need to get the dragon back," blushes the dragon rider.

"No worries, Pete," says Connor, swinging his leg round and agilely jumping to the ground.

My body is stiff from the cold and my holding it tensely. I somehow manage to swing my leg over the dragon's back and slide off its wing on my backside.

Connor holds his hands out to me and pulls me to my feet.

"Easy now. I've got you."

My legs are left shaking now that the adrenaline rush has left my body. Connor has to grab me round the waist to keep me standing. He walks me steadily over to a rug next to a tree where I collapse. Connor gives the dragon something to eat and a pat, shakes the hand of the dragon rider and takes a backpack off him before waving as they take off and disappear. We are utterly alone.

I close my eyes and lift my face to the sun, willing my land sickness to subside. I hear the clink of a metal flask.

"This will help." He puts a mug in my hand. My eyes open in shock and I start to cough. I was expecting the ubiquitous cup of tea. Connor is hunkered in front of me laughing.

"It wasn't that funny."

"It was."

"What is it, anyway?" I sniff the mug.

"Hot toddy. It's the drink of choice after a dragon ride. It'll warm you up and settle your stomach." I bring the mug to my lips and take another drink. The whiskey warms my belly. The lemon and honey disguise the whisky taste and perk me up. A couple of swigs and I'm done.

I hold out my mug to Connor who is stretched out beside me sipping his drink slowly.

"Easy tiger. Let's get some food in you first." He hands me some sort of green leafy wrap. I pick off the decorative flowers.

"You eat those."

I freeze. Throwing away flowers in the Flowerlands probably isn't good date etiquette.

"Hmm," I bring the purple flowers to my mouth. "Yum," I'm proud of how convincing I sound. I chew cautiously. Actually it *is* yummy.

I'm so hungry I eat that one then inhale a couple more. Fresh air does that to me. Fish and chips at the seaside. Hot Toddy and green-nutty-floral-wraps dragon riding.

My legs have stopped shaking and I'm feeling relaxed and mellow. Connor is lying on the blanket, arms behind his head. I shuffle down and prop myself up on my elbow beside him. Muscles relaxed, face free of responsibility, he's even more of a demi-god. He opens his eyes and catches my blatant ogling. Our eyes lock. The pull is immediate. My hair sprawls around us as I lean down. Connor sweeps my hair back over my shoulder before cupping the back of my head. A millimeter from Connor's lips my breath hitches. Finally!

"Good ride?" Our foreheads clatter against each other as Connor jerks up. "Dragon riding leaves me a little frisky too. All that adrenaline." My face turns scarlet. Lucien turns and walks back into the tree line. I clutch my head.

"Aarrrggggghhhh," groans Connor, flopping back and covering his eyes.

"Oh my God." I gasp as my blurred vision clears.

We are surrounded by curious fae munching popping dandelion puffs. Watching us like we're the evening entertainment. I drop my hand from my head and narrow my eyes at a couple Sprites. *Are they taking bets?* Connor is on his feet, pulling me to him as the crowd closes in. It seems that everyone wants to look at me. Connor is jostled out the way. I'm goggled and stared at and poked and prodded. Faeries have no shame! They blatantly discuss my features with each other. They touch my hair, stroke my skin, pinch my cheeks. One even poked me in the stomach, repeatedly until Connor lifted her finger away. I've a bit more flesh than most faeries, but still.

"Can we go?" I ask in a lull between gawkers.

"Yeah." Connor takes my elbow firmly. The crowd move back as Connor treats them to a 'don't even think about it' look. His body on-point ready to guard.

We stride back to the castle in a cloud of tension.

"I'll get the kitchen to bring you some ice, lump should go down by tomorrow." His jaw clicks as he gingerly runs his fingers over the swelling. "Well, goodnight," he says, and turns to leave.

"Connor." He stills when I put my hand on his arm. "I'm sorry."

"It wasn't your fault."

"No, but it feels that way. I had a great time tonight, I would have had a greater time without the interruption." I frown remembering the shocking lack of manners. "It was my first ever date."

"Yeah?" He looks pleased with himself. "Then I'm sorry your first date was the worst first date in the history of first dates."

I can't help but laugh.

"Look on the bright side. It can only get better, right? Can we do it again sometime?"

He sighs. "I don't know, Lucy."

He turns and disappears into the darkness.

CHAPTER TWENTY-SIX

I toss and turn all night, and so when the sun rises I decide to join it. I make it to the clearing in time for mediation and manage to sit still for the entire session. Imogen comes over afterwards and we climb to the Emerald Loch. My quad muscles are trembling in outraged agony by the time we reach the top.

"That was harder than I expected." I wipe sweat from my brow with the back of my hand.

"It'll take time for your body to readjust." I fill my lungs with cool clear air.

"Why are we here?"

"Mirror work."

I frown.

"We've done that already."

"Not with this body."

"Why do we need to come here to do mirror work when there are mirrors in the castle?"

"Well, it's fantastic exercise coming up here. The views are spectacular. Don't you agree?"

"And?"

"And you get privacy to do what you need to do. OK, let's begin."

I step over to the water's edge, kneel down and place my hands beside my knees to support me. Tiny pieces of gravel dig into my knees and palms. The water is flat today, only the tiniest ripples caused by fish here and there.

I begin to look at my reflection. I am so pleased to see my face again. My otherwise pale skin pink from the exertion of the climb. My hair is blonder, wavier and longer than I remember it. My face isn't as fat as I thought, my cheek bones more defined. My eyes bluer. I never thought I would be able to look at myself in the mirror, never mind be enchanted with what I see.

I look deep into my eyes. I really look this time, my eyes don't just skirt and skim. I look and look. "You are beautiful. I love you," I say to my reflection. To my surprise, tears of joy prick my eyes. "I love you, I really love you," I laugh. I stand, brushing off the tiny stones stuck to my knees and hands. I skip over to Imogen, grab her hands and spin her in a circle.

"Imogen, you are beautiful. I love you. I really love you." I start to speed up. We are both laughing.

"Imogen, I am beautiful. I love myself." We are spinning so far out that we both lose our balance and land on our backs on the ground. We lie next to each, laughing at the sky. Turning to each other and laughing harder until we cry.

It is nice seeing Imogen so young and carefree. She is so wise I sometimes forget that Imogen is nearly the same age as me. She has the responsibility of looking after a kingdom. Not just physically, making sure they are safe and well with enough to eat, but spiritually too. She looks so happy I'm glad she has Dylan. He's not as insubstantial as I first thought. He's strong enough for Imogen to lean on. He's as spiritual as she is albeit his is an earthy spirituality, whilst hers is more ethereal. His cheerfulness and good humor will keep her light; stop her being pulled down by responsibility.

"What is it?" she says when she sees me staring.

"Nothing really. I'm just happy for you. You and Dylan are so well matched. I think you'll have a great life together."

"Life doesn't come with a guarantee, but I think we will too."

"And have beautiful babies?"

"Sooner rather than later." She grins.

"OMG! You're pregnant?"

She tries to hide her grin, but her lips aren't listening. "A honeymoon baby is expected. After all, that's why they want us married."

"You have to be married to have babies? That's a little archaic, isn't it?"

"No, we don't need to be married to have babies but the elders do want guarantees and a marriage is the best way to ensure that. Marriages here aren't the same as yours. Couples commit to each other for a period. If they wish to remain married, they renew their vows. If they don't, they are released from their vows. For the couples that were only meant to be together for a short time, there is no trauma of divorce. For the couples that stay together, they get to recommit to each other often.

"Anyway, enough about me. Let's get on."

I look up at Imogen.

"What now?"

"Now you get naked."

My screech is so high I scratch my throat.

"Are you crazy? I'm not taking my clothes off." I fold my arms over my chest and frown.

"You have to do this. Time is running out for all of us." Imogen gives an exasperated sigh. "Do you want to go home?"

I open my mouth to answer but nothing comes out.

CHAPTER TWENTY-SEVEN

Keeping my back to Imogen, I take off my newly scuffed boots, tucking my socks inside. I lay my dress with reverence on the boulder. I raise my arms behind my back to unhook my bra and step out of the matching lavender silk and fuchsia lace panties. I cover my breasts with one hand and my vagina with the other and wince as I tiptoe over tiny pebbles to Imogen at the water's edge.

"Now what?"

"You do the same thing again. This time with your whole body, not just your face." I gingerly step to the edge until the freezing water is lapping my toes. I take a deep breath. Drop my hands to my sides and lower my eyes to my reflection. I immediately step back and turn to Imogen, modesty forgotten.

"I can't do it! Why can't I do it? I could do it as an elephant. Why can't I do it like this?"

"It's OK, Lucy. Any sort of healing happens in layers. Like an onion, you peel one layer off to get to the next layer. You have pulled quite a few layers off in the last few months. But you have been criticizing your body for a long time. All that has happened just now is that you looked at yourself and the negative comments came to the surface. This is a good thing. Sometimes you have to open a wound to let the infection out and to allow it to heal. That's all that has happened here. Do you want to try again?"

I sigh and step determinedly to the water.

"OK, Lucy, when you are ready lower your eyes to look at your reflection. Keep looking at your reflection until you are connected to it. And let me know when that has happened." Imogen's voice is soft and hypnotic.

"Now, I would like you to look at your toes and say *my toes are beautiful. I love my toes.*"

"My toes are beautiful. I love my toes," I say.

"Now your feet."

"My feet are beautiful. I love my feet."

"Now work your way up your body: ankles, shins, thighs and so on."

"My ankles are beautiful. I love my ankles."

"My shins are beautiful. I love my shins."

"My calves are beautiful. I love my calves."

"My thighs are beautiful. I love my thighs." My nose wrinkles.

"What just happened?" says Imogen.

"I'm not feeling the love for my thighs today or any day for that matter."

"Just keep repeating *my thighs are beautiful. I love my thighs*, until you feel comfortable enough to move on," says Imogen.

"My thighs are beautiful. I love my thighs." I have to say this many times before I can move on to my hips, bottom, stomach – again, repeating several times – ribs, breasts, chest, arms, shoulders, neck, face, lips, nose, ears, eyes and finally hair.

"Great work. Now say to yourself, *my body is beautiful. I love my body.*"

"My body is beautiful. I love my body." To my surprise, it feels OK. But I'm aiming for great.

"I think that is enough for now. Well done! Come and have lunch," says Imogen. I turn and there is rug and a hamper.

"Who brought lunch?"

"Connor, of course."

"He was here?" I squeak.

But Imogen has already walked away to prepare lunch. With the day being so hot, the salad she is dishing up is welcome. I look around furtively and dress quickly in case there is anybody else about.

"Why do you keep forcing me to look in a mirror anyway?" I say, forking a yellow flower into my mouth.

"Mirror work is crucial for self-acceptance as most people ignore what's really there. When we look in the mirror for any length of time, we cannot help but see what is. People berate themselves all the time, measuring themselves on other people's expectations. They never really ask themselves who am I? Who can I become? If I could do anything, what would I do? If I could have anything in this world what would it be? Truth is, most people don't really want to dream because they don't believe it is possible for dreams to come true.

"Have you heard of an aura?" Mouth full, I nod. "Contained within our aura we have four ethereal bodies:

body, mind, emotional and spiritual. If one of those is out of balance, it affects the whole. To be truly and completely whole, all four bodies need to be in alignment.

"With positive affirmations you told your **mind** you are good enough, loved and loveable.

The clothed mirror work tells your **emotions** that you are good enough, loved and loveable. You're connecting with your heart that already knows you are loved, loveable, good enough and beautiful exactly as you are.

"Naked mirror work connects you with your **body**. Most people dislike something about their body and some people hate parts, if not all, of their body. The body is your temple whist you are on this earth.

"What unclothed mirror work does is allow you to connect with our body again. It allows you to appreciate your own beauty. Every body is different and there lies the secret. The beauty is not because we are all the same but because we are all different. The beauty is in the diversity.

"Another little exercise to try is finding one thing you like about yourself every time you look in the mirror. It can be *my hair is nice today, my skin looks good, and my make-up really brings out the beauty of my eyes*. If you can find more than one thing, even better. If you can find three things then you are really advanced," laughs Imogen.

"What about the spiritual body?"

"We'll get to that. Now, let's get out of here. I have a wedding to organize."

CHAPTER TWENTY-EIGHT

Smoke is billowing from the chimney, so I head through the wide-open forge door instead of my own private studio entrance. Connor is stripped to the waist, muscles rippling and flexing as he tends something in the fire. It is a scorching summer's day, the hottest it's been. His damp hair is clinging to the back of his neck. I suddenly have a desire to lick the sweat off his naked back. *OMG!* I look away before my warped mind can come up with anything more disgusting.

"Hey." He's turned his head to look at me.

I can't look at him between the thoughts of his naked body and knowing that he has seen mine. I flee into my studio. Banging the door shut, I lean against it breathing deeply to try to slow my racing heart. Suddenly the door moves and I'm stumbling backwards – only a pair of strong arms stops me crashing to the floor. Unfortunately, well later it might seem fortunate, Connor's hands land on my breasts as he steadies me.

"Sorry about that." His eyes drop to my chest. I don't know which one of us is more embarrassed.

"Did you want something?"

"Yeah, I just wanted to check you were OK. You seemed a little off when you came in."

My eyes lock onto his naked chest. Desire swamps me again. My legs cross at the ankles. I clench my hands to resist reaching out to glide them over his glistening body before following with my lips.

"No, I'm fine," I squeak before clearing my throat. "I just came to get some supplies. I'm going to paint the hustle and bustle."

"Let me know if you need a hand." He beams at me. His hands were doing just fine a moment ago.

I sigh and nearly whimper as he walks to his workbench and picks up a hammer.

I pack my satchel and head for the village. The lights of an apartment block that catch my attention. Candlelight illuminates the underside of the leaves. I decide to start there. I count fifteen homes, up and around the copper beech. The windows are formed out of tree knots. A few have platforms outside like balconies. The windows are decorated with moss and climbing flowers. There are a couple of swings spread throughout the high branches where the faeries hang and watch the hubbub. There are a few mushroom and acorn houses scattered round the base of the tree all linked by a trellised walkway heavy with scented blooms.

I pack everything away and carefully carry the oil painting back to the studio. I put the canvas on an easel and clean off my brushes. I leave through the forge. The fire is banked and it's disappointingly empty.

*

Imogen accosts me as soon as I enter the castle.

"Your dinner is in the dining room, Lucy."

"I'm not really hungry just now. Can I have it later?"

"Certainly. Is there anything else I can do for you?"

"Actually, there is. Is it possible to have a hot bath?"

It turns out there is a bathing chamber three doors down from my bedroom that no one thought to tell me about. I hurry upstairs, take my clothes off and slip into my dressing gown. My clothes disappear every night and reappear clean every morning.

As I step out of my room, I hear the *slap, slap* of feet against the wood. I follow the noise to see a bright green tail disappear into the bathing chamber. Curious, I follow. The door opens with a haunted squeak. On the edge of the sunken bath tiled in gold mosaics is a baby dragon breathing fire onto the water. When it stops, a faerie is swirling the water around with a stick. Then the dragon breathes again. This goes on until the temperature is just right.

I walk over and the dragon's tongue laps my hand. "He likes you," says the faerie. I run my hand over the little green dragon's back. He is surprisingly soft. He purrs as I scratch behind his ears before he is led away by the collar and I sink gratefully into the hot water. Aches and pains melt away.

I wrap myself in a silk dressing gown and glide my hands over the fabric. It's short, only just covering my bottom, so I hurry back to my bedroom before anyone can see me. It appeared the same night I morphed back to me, along with a silk and lace negligee thing that I would die if anyone saw me wearing. I must talk to Tatiana about making jammies.

I reach to get my nightie from under my pillow. It's not there. It's been washed and pressed again and hung on the back of the door. A bright blue glass bottle is on the nightstand that wasn't there before my bath. Curious, I pick it up and lift it to the light. The label reads *lovingly massage into skin*. I screw the lid off and smell. Oh my, it smells divine. I pour a little onto the tips of my fingers. I put the open bottle on the nightstand and move to lock my door. I slip my dressing gown off, pick up the massage oil and pour some into my hands.

Instinctively I rub my hands together until the oil is warm and fluid. I put one foot up on my wooden stool and begin stroking from my toes, over my ankles, calves, thighs. I repeat *I love my toes etc.* as I make my way up my body. I pour a little more oil and change legs. A little more oil and I massage over my arms. A little more oil and I stroke both my hands over my bottom and round to my stomach, round to my lower back, over my ribs. It feels lovely, kind of hypnotic and relaxing. At least, it is until I get further up. As I move my hands over my breasts, my nipples harden and I start breathing a little more quickly. I get butterflies in my tummy and I start tingling further down. I stop immediately and cap the bottle. I fling my nightgown on and jump into bed, pulling the covers over me. What is happening to me? First inappropriate fantasies about Connor, now this. I narrow my eyes suspiciously at the bottle.

CHAPTER TWENTY-NINE

I find myself settling into a routine. Up early, hike to the emerald loch. Tell myself I love myself. Spend the afternoons painting or drawing. Lovingly massage my exhausted body. Then conk out.

I feel amazing. All the fresh air and exercise. My muscles are happy from the daily climb. I am less pale from being outdoors all the time. I am eating nothing but healthy food. OK, with a cake or two thrown in – it's law in these parts, in the faerie handbook under *have your cake and enjoy it* section. And I love, love, love painting every day.

I have decided to paint a book. Not an actual book, but a series of oils depicting life in the Flowerlands. It's kind of cool because I get to do landscapes and portraits. I've finished the summer meadows showing the flowers and their faeries. I've painted the bluebell woods from memory. I've painted the children playing in the river. I've got loads of ideas. I've started a portrait of Dylan and Imogen that I'll give to them for a wedding present. I want to paint the bakery and Joe and Joni because I love it and them. I want to paint the trees with the hobbits, the pixies and wood nymphs. The main street with all its shops. Dylan and

Lucien competing and the dragons. The castle, the banquets, the morning meditation. I want to paint the Protectors training and working. I want to paint the four kings and queens laughing together. I want to paint the forge and Connor, especially Connor. I want to paint everything that tells the story of my life here. It will take me months, maybe even years. I am getting the basics down on canvas so that I can work on the paintings through the winter. From what I can gather, things are dead here in winter.

The leaves are beginning to turn when I am ready to paint the Emerald Loch. I decide to stay up here few days. Connor has come with me.

Mostly, I sit in my chair and paint the landscape. The loch as it glows emerald in the sun. The still water that looks like sky. The shallow aquamarine edges where you can see the stony bottom and fish darting across. The hills opposite that reflect dark jagged peaks on the other side of the water. The blue sky with little fluffy clouds. When I pick up my brushes, I disappear for hours. I am in another place altogether.

Connor makes me take breaks every so often. Instinctively, he knows when it's OK to disturb me. Otherwise he rolls up his trousers and walks barefoot into the water, standing motionless until he has speared a fish. Or he sits silently meditating. Well, not meditating exactly. He spends hours sending healing energy out into the world. There's not much to see, but it's still impressive to watch.

Connor does everything. He prepares our beds. Washes

the clothes. Lays the fire. Makes the tea. Forages and gathers. Cooks lunch and dinner. Sings to me. It has been a long time since anyone took care of me like this. My parents are busy and leave me to my own devices. I like how Connor likes taking care of me, asking nothing in return, leaving me completely free to do what I need to do. Never an imposition, just treasured and protected.

We sleep side by side each night in sleeping bags in the cave behind the loch, where I move my canvas at the end of the day to keep the canvas dry and let the paint dry. Yet he hasn't even tried to kiss me. I have sneaked my hand close to his a few times so that our pinkies are nearly touching. A centimeter more and we would be holding hands. I'm not brave enough to try. I'm hoping he'll kiss me soon. There are only so many times I can maneuver myself with my lips tilted to Connor before it moves beyond embarrassing and into desperation.

Three days after we arrive, Dylan and Imogen bring fresh supplies.

"Getting much done?" asks Dylan, wiggling his eyebrows. Connor and I look away from each other.

"Dylan!" laughs Imogen. It's not funny.

"Yes, lots," I say.

"How much longer will you be?"

"I should finish painting today. The canvas will be dry enough to carry back to my studio tomorrow."

"Lucien needs you to return and prepare the hunt," says Imogen to Connor.

"What about Lucy?"

"Dylan can stay with her."

"NO!" he snaps.

Imogen stares at Connor.

"I don't believe that's your decision to make, is it Lieutenant?"

His jaw muscles bunch. But he doesn't argue.

Imogen continues to stare, before sighing.

"Dylan, I think it would be best if I stayed with Lucy. We have some more work to do."

"No!" says Dylan, folding his arms over his chest.

"No?" Imogen arches an imperial eyebrow at him.

"There's no one to protect you."

"I'm a big girl. I can protect myself. Besides I need some time away from all the wedding planning and preparation. It will be nice to spend some time with my best girl."

"OK," he mumbles, moving in to kiss Imogen. They are too unguarded and intimate to watch. I look to Connor. He is glaring at them.

"For god's sake, give it a rest will you," says Connor. He turns on his heel and marches off. Dylan and Imogen pull apart to watch him.

"Excuse me," I say, putting my head down. I don't know why I'm ashamed. I'm not the one being rude.

I follow him into the cave where he is stuffing his spare clothes into his duffel bag. He glances at me when my shadow falls over him, but says nothing.

"Are you angry with me?"

"No!"

"Then why are you being this way?"

"What way?" He stands and flings his duffel over his shoulder.

"All prickly and prudish."

"You think I'm a prude?" His voice scales a few octaves.

"Well, aren't you?"

His mouth opens and closes a few times before he turns and storms out the cave, without a backwards glance.

After a few moments, Imogen enters.

"Did you want something?"

"Yes, I have another exercise for you to try. Shall we do it outside? Dylan has laid out a quilt."

Imogen directs me to lie down and get comfortable on the blanket as she kneels beside me. I wriggle about until I find a position where there isn't a stone digging into me. I bend my knees and lift my bottom, smoothing my dress under me. When I am settled, Imogen covers me in another blanket and tucks me in.

"You might get cold during this."

"What are we doing?"

"I am going to take you on an inner journey. Your body has an innate intelligence, it knows what's good for it. I'm going to show you how to access that information for yourself. To call on your guides and helpers to hold you and protect you during this journey.

"When you were born you were assigned spirit guides to support you through your life. You have a spirit animal such as a horse or wolf or bird or elephant. Your power animal represents the whole breed; it isn't just a single animal. The animal will have attributes that are important to you. It is important to remember a mouse is no less powerful than a lion. You also have a guide or teacher with you. Sometimes it's a loved one who has passed or it could be an angel or a past master. These helping spirits guide you and love and protect you. I will show you how to journey to meet your spirit guides another time. All you need to know just now is to ask for them to come close. So, go ahead and call your guides. Ask them, out loud or in your head, to surround you and keep you safe during this journey."

I close my eyes, then fling my arm over them to block out the daylight.

"Begin to relax, going deeper and deeper, getting more and more relaxed with each breath you take. You are going to step down a flight of ten steps and when you reach the bottom you will find yourself at your favorite place in nature. It could be a waterfall, a cave, a forest, a beach, or a park. Ten getting deeper and deeper, nine stepping down getting more and more relaxed … eight going deeper and deeper … seven getting more and more relaxed … six going deeper and deeper … five getting more and more relaxed ………. four going deeper and deeper ………. three … getting … more … and … more … relaxed ……………… two going … deeper … and … deeper ……………………………. and …… one ………. stepping into your favorite place in nature.

"Look around. Do you see anything? Maybe you feel rather than see, or maybe you can hear things. Or maybe you smell or taste. Or maybe your gut will give you answers. Take a few moments to see what you see, hear what you hear and feel what you feel.

"Now, I would like you to ask your body to come to you. When an object approaches you, ask it: are you my body? If it says no, thank it for coming and wait for the next object to approach. Your body could look how you look or take the form of an animal or an angel or a mythical creature, a tree, a mountain or whatever. Just trust that whatever comes is right for you."

I nod my understanding, so relaxed I can't speak.

A large oak tree approaches me. I ask it – are you my body? I hear the word *Yes* in my head. I'm a bit miffed. I wanted a ballerina or a runner, something lithe and graceful, not a great big sturdy tree. Why am I a tree? I ask it. *Oak trees are strong, we can withstand almost anything. Our roots go deep into the earth so we can take great nourishment. We have great balance; our roots are in the earth and our branches close to heaven.* I'm not sure what all that means, but it sounds good.

Guided by Imogen, I ask, *how can I take the best possible care of you?* Two branches come out of the side of the tree like arms. The tree begins to sway and move. Then it's twirling. It comes over and takes my arms and starts waltzing me around. You want me to dance? *Yes*, says the tree. Then it starts bending over and touching its toes. Then it goes into a series of weird positions. Yoga, you're doing yoga! I giggle at the yogi tree. Then it's holding its arms round its waist and miming laughing. You want me to laugh more? The tree nods, then swirls its hands around waiting for more. And enjoy life more? *Exactly* it says, *and don't take life so seriously*. OK. Then it sweeps its arm along and a table appears covered in food. There is a small amount of steak, a little chicken, fish, nuts, seeds, legumes, a few grains and rice. Loads of different fruit and veg in all colors of the rainbow. Some dairy. Some cake and chocolate – yay. Then at the end there is a small corner with take-out foods and a few sweets. This is what you want me to eat? *Yes, fresh natural foods as much as possible. Home cooked. Organic where possible. Take out or junk food is OK in moderation.* I frown. I'll try, but it's quite a change. *Not really, you have been living this way in the Flowerlands. You've enjoyed it, haven't you?* Well yeah, but I didn't have a choice. *You don't have to do it all at once, baby steps and you will get there. You have been living this way, just carry on this way and it will be easy.* OK, I'll try, but I'm not promising anything.

"OK Lucy," Imogen's voice breaks into my thoughts. "Thank your body for the information and thank your helpers and guides. Turn around and come back the way you came. As you climb each step you are becoming lighter and lighter and more and more awake. Ten, nine, eight, seven, six, five waking up now, four, three, two and one: opening your eyes feeling fresh and energized."

I pop my eyes open and look around in a daze.

"I feel a little out of it."

"Stand up and take your tights off. Walking barefoot in the grass will help ground you or if you are in a place where you can't walk on the grass imagine roots growing deep into the earth."

I strip my tights off and pad about the dry grass until I am fully awake and back in my body.

CHAPTER THIRTY

As the sun sets, the temperature plummets. Imogen and I make for the cave and light a fire. I give my sleeping bag to Imogen. I use Connor's. It smells of him: fire, outdoors and hard work.

"Umm, so what do we do now?" says Imogen, looking awkward.

"You've never had sleepovers?"

She shakes her head.

"No, I don't really have close friends, except Dylan." She smiles. "Don't get me wrong, fae are lovely, but they don't let their hair down with me. It makes it hard to have friends. It's one of the reasons I'm glad you're here." She leans over and squeezes my hand. "Have you had many sleepovers?"

"Not so many lately. My best friend Daisy is an epic genius and doesn't really have time for frivolity. My other friend Gordon, well, sleepovers just wouldn't work with him. I used to have great girls nights with my mum and my gran and my aunt Claire. My aunt and gran would come over and stay and they would make cocktails. They would paint each other's toes or give each other facials or try out different make up. There would be fashion shows, mostly by mum. Then they would make popcorn and watch a chick flick gossiping. I got to stay up with them."

"You don't do it now?"

"No." Just thinking about makes me sad. "Gran died and my mum and aunt are busy with work so it kind of died out."

"Umm…in the spirit of female bonding," says Imogen, wringing her hands.

"Yes," I freeze. A nervous Imogen is making me nervous.

"Well, I was wondering if you would like to be my bridesmaid?" she says quietly. Her cheeks turn a lovely rose pink.

"Really?" I beam at her. She nods her head shyly. I clap my hands excitedly. "Yay!" I dive on her and hug her tightly. "Are you sure?" She nods. "I've never been a bridesmaid before."

"We've never had a bridesmaid before. Faeries don't normally have bridesmaids but I've always liked that human tradition. Sometimes it's good to be queen." She beams.

Suddenly cold, I climb into my sleeping bag. Imogen copies me and we lie on our sides facing each other, our faces lit by the glowing fire. "So, what about you and Connor?"

I sigh heavily.

"I really don't know what to make of him, Imogen. One minute he's giving out signals that he really likes me and the next he's so standoffish that I think I imagined it. I mean we were alone for days and he never tried anything. Absolutely nothing." I huff and flop back onto my sleeping bag.

"Hmm, maybe he didn't like the other Protectors watching."

"We were being watched?" I squeak. Oh my god. I was naked.

"Imogen, can I ask you something?" I lean up on my elbow and look at the fire.

"I think there's something wrong with me."

Her smile drops from her face.

"Oh?"

"I keep having these visions, well fantasies, about Connor."

I blush scarlet, avoiding eye contact. I tell her about the forge.

"Where I… strip him and then you know. And then we… you know, in the studio or in the woods or in the meadows well not the summer meadows because there are too many folks watching. And then there is going into the river to cool off. Only we don't cool off."

"Is that all?" Imogen is laughing at me.

"What do you mean, is that all?"

"I thought you were going to tell me something else."

"Did you have fantasies about Dylan?"

"Oh yes! For five years. I couldn't look at him for the first year without going scarlet. It's normal when you are in love with someone."

"I'm not in…Oh no." I flop back again and hit the heel of my hand against my forehead. "How did that happen?"

"You've spent a lot of time with an incredible man. Not only is he ridiculously handsome, he's also kind and honorable. I've known him all his life. He takes his work seriously and he doesn't fool around."

"That's good to know."

"His family are like wolves. They seek their soul mate and when they mate, they mate for life."

"Why has he been sleeping outside my bedroom?"

"He was protecting you. There are some people who – *well*, let's just say they weren't happy he brought you here."

"Connor brought me here?"

"Yes, he's the one that found you. He came back and convinced us that you were who we were looking for. He feels responsible because of it. Like I said, he takes his work very seriously." Imogen gets up and banks the fire.

"Is it me they don't like?"

"No, it's having a human here. You're the first and probably the last."

Without another word, she turns over and goes to sleep.

I sleep but my dreams are full of piercing blue eyes, wolves and warriors protecting me from unseen enemies.

CHAPTER THIRTY-ONE

Next morning, I head straight for the forge. It's empty. The fire is cold. I go into my studio and pretend to work. I tidy and clean. Hang the canvases I am working on so that they are off the ground away from possible damage. I start grinding rock to make new paints.

Connor doesn't appear that day or the next day or the day after that. I repeatedly walk past the training grounds. He's never there. On the third day, I head to the common room at the barracks. I'm directed to a room that conveniently has Connor in wooden letters upon it. I knock. No answer. I put my ear to the door and listen. Nothing. I turn the door handle and the door eases open.

I walk into a small neat room. There is a wooden single bed with a black quilt over it and a pillow. There is a bedside table with a candle on it, a chest of drawers a wardrobe and a full-length mirror on the back of the door. I peek out into the corridor to see if anybody is about before opening the wardrobe. There are a few everyday uniforms, his dress uniform, a black duffel coat and a pair of shiny black boots as well as few shirts and a beautiful grey silk suit.

I sneakily begin opening his drawers. White and black cotton boxer shorts in the underwear drawer. A drawer of T-shirts, another with a few pairs of jeans. The next drawer has sweaters, a couple of cashmere V-necks and hoodies. I lift it out to see if it smells of him.

"Can I help you?" drawls a male voice. I scream and raise my hand to my chest.

"Lucien, you scared me." He arches his brow at me. "Um ...I was looking for Connor."

"Well, he isn't in that drawer." I realize I'm still holding Connor's hoodie. I stuff it in the drawer and ram it shut.

"No...well. Do you know where he is?"

"Yes." It's my turn to arch my brow.

"When will he be back?" I say softly.

He lifts one shoulder as he regards me dispassionately.

"Why are you doing this?"

He regards me with a hard glint. "To protect him of course."

"Who from?"

His lips quirk. "You."

I gasp. "I'm not going to hurt Connor."

"You sure about that? What happens when you leave here and go back to mummy and daddy and Connor is left broken-hearted, made to look a fool in front of everyone he knows?"

"I'm going home?" I whisper. What if I get sent home before Connor returns? I might never see him again.

"Let's hope so, hmm?"

*

I'm four rungs up a ladder trying to figure out what's missing from my wedding present. It needs something but I'm scared to touch it incase I ruin the whole thing. I lean over to try a tiny dab of copper paint. Perfect! I'm trying another when a noise at the studio door startles me off the ladder. A firm pair of hands reach me before a reach the floor.

"Connor!" I'm pressed hard against him until he steps back.

"Steady." He keeps ahold of my elbows. "OK?" I nod. "When did you get back?"

"Just now."

I would be struggling to breathe only I want to inhale as much of that fresh air and man scent as I can. We stare at each other.

"The hunt's tomorrow."

"What are you hunting for?"

"The Wedding Feast. I thought you might like to experience catching your supper. Actually it was Tatiana's idea."

My nose scrunches up. "Meat comes plastic wrapped from a supermarket where I come from and that's the way I like it."

"I can teach you how to use a bow and arrow." He looks like a puppy waiting for someone to kick a ball. It's adorable.

"Oh OK then."

We trail our way through the knee-high wild flowers. Connor has a pouch with dozens of arrows strapped to his back.

He's carrying a bow that looks like a sideways handlebar mustache tied with a piece of string. We stop about half way down the summer meadows and turn to face a large oak tree. There's a round piece of wood strapped to it with multi-colored concentric circles painted on it.

Connor straps a piece of leather to his wrist. "Watch and learn." He pulls an arrow from the pouch, arranges it, pulls back the string and fires. Bulls-eye.

"Your turn." He grins smugly at me. He removes the leather from around his wrist and straps it to mine. Pulls an arrow from the pouch and hands it to me along with the bow. I try to balance the arrow the way Connor did but it's not co-operating.

"Other way."

"Huh." I purse my lips at the bow.

"Let me show you." He comes to stand behind me smelling of wind dried laundry. He takes the bow turns it so the mustache is at the front and the string at the back. Takes the arrow and rests it on a little wooden ledge in the middle of the mustache. Then places the quiver in the string.

"Raise the bow until your right arm is straight and your left arm is parallel to the ground." He places one hand on my right shoulder whilst the finger of his left hand caresses the sensitive skin of the inside of my left elbow.

"Now pull the string back like this." He whispers softly against the shell of my ear as he pulls my left arm back. "Now release." His fingers drop away. I'm so disappointed I fail to notice the arrow lying offensively at my feet.

"Oh."

"You need more tension." *I really don't!* "Try again." He

feeds me arrows again and again. They land at my feet, in the trees, fly wildly to my left and to my right. It's only when I stop to go and retrieve the missing arrows that I notice the faeries have retreated from their flowers in the shadows of the trees. We only recover half of what I shot. I narrow my eyes accusingly at the laughing crowd, trying to see who has hidden them.

Connor hands me another arrow and comes to stand beside me again. The shots begin to go straight and get closer and closer to the target. Finally when my arm muscles are burning in protest and the blister on my middle finger has burst I hit the outer circle.

I scream with delight. "Did you see that?" I beam. "I did it. I actually did it!" I begin to dance a victory dance. "I did it!" Crazy arms, "I did it." Turn and shake my butt at Connor. "I really, really did it." I stop when I see Connor's utter bemusement at my dancing. I turn scarlet.

"Not bad for a beginner eh?"

"Not bad at all. Now let's do it for real." He takes my hand and pulls me behind him.

"What do you mean?"

"You're going to catch your supper."

"No. I can't." I pull hard on his hand.

"Yes. You. Can." He stops and tugs me to him. "Hunting is the only way to eat meat round here. You've been eating meat haven't you?" I nod. "This is more honest that plastic wrapped frightened animals isn't it?"

"I guess." I grumble.

"I prayed for an animal to give up its life for us before we set out today and I'll leave an offering as thanks when we are finished." He takes my face in his hands and bends down and rubs his nose against mine. "OK?"

I nod once. We walk side by side. I try to smother my ecstatic smile when he slings his arm over my shoulder but I can't.

"Look, there we go," he whispers as he points. He slowly unsheathes an arrow. I look around but can only see stones. Then one stone moves and there is a little white pom-pom. Connor tries to hand me the bow. I shake my head at him. He smiles encouragingly and thrusts the bow at me. I take it, then the arrow. I place the arrow in the bow and raise my arms.

"Nooooooo," I shout.

"You did it." Connor beams at me, lifts me up and spins me around. The only shot I've tried to miss all day. Connor has lifted it up by the ears.

"It's a clean shot." Right between the eyes. He notices my eyes. "It died instantly Lucy. No pain."

"How do you know?"

He's kneeling beside the rabbit brandishing a knife. "I just do."

I kneel beside him. "But it's so fluffy and soft," I say, stroking the pelt.

"Yeah I know. It'll make a great hat or boot lining." He makes incisions with his knife. Then he starts pulling the fur off.

"STOP! Oh God please stop." I turn my back to Connor and lose my lunch.

"Lucy?" Connor places a hand on my shoulder. I turn my head. His hand is covered in blood.

"Oh God."

I run and run and run. My lungs are on the verge of spontaneous combustion when I burst through the castle doors.

"Lucy?" says Imogen coming out of the banquet hall.

"Not now."

I take the stairs two at a time. I slam and lock the door of my room before curling up on my bed.

A soft rap startles me.

"It's me." Connor's voice is muffled through the door. He knocks again. I stay still as...well a rabbit hiding in a field.

"Lucy?" He knocks gently again. "I'm sorry OK?" I think it's his forehead that *thunks* against the door. "I didn't mean to freak you out. It's just...I didn't think." He taps the door again. "Talk to me, Lucy." He sighs. "Can you at least let me know you are alive?" My tongues refuses to work. "I'm going to count to five and if I don't hear anything I'm coming in. Five. Four. Three…"

"Go away!"

CHAPTER THIRTY-TWO

I wake with a start. It's pitch dark. Jumping out of bed, I fumble about on the floor for my clothes lying where I dropped them last night. Fierce rain is bouncing off the ground. I stumble and trip repeatedly without the moon to guide me.

I pick up a stone and throw, hoping to God I don't hit Lucien's window. I didn't do so well with hitting or missing intended targets today. *Pink.* I do it again. *Pink.*

"What the…" says a sleepy Connor with total bed head.

"*Psst* Connor." He peers through the sheeting rain.

"Lucy?"

"Shhh!" I hiss.

"What are you doing here?" His head disappears. I glimpse a naked back before it's covered in a clinging black shirt. His head appears again. "I'm coming down."

The door opens and I hurl myself into his arms and hold on tight. He holds the back of my head as I bury my face in his neck.

"I had a…"

"Wait." He puts his fingers to my lips and whispers against my ear. "Let's not chance waking Lucien."

I let go and we creep stealthily away. Him more than me. Connor leads me upstairs to my bedroom. He lights the fire, hands me a towel then leaves. I dry myself, pick my nightie from where I threw it earlier and quickly put it on before climbing into bed.

He comes back with two steaming cups of cocoa, placing them on the bedside cabinet so that he can pick my clothes up from the wet heap on the floor lay them out in front of the fire. Before toweling himself with the damp towel.

He picks the mugs up and hands one to me then sits cross-legged at the bottom of my bed.

"Want to tell me what happened?" he says softly, blowing on his drink.

I swallow. Hard.

"I had a dream that I was being hunted. I was running through the woods. I was totally out of breath but I couldn't stop. I could feel whoever it was behind me getting closer. I get too tired to run, I stumble and decide to rest against a tree. The snapping of a twig makes me look up. There is something coming straight at me and suddenly there is a bow and arrow in my hands. I raise it and fire. It's a clean shot right through the heart."

"A larger than life fluffy bunny?" he says.

"No. It was you."

"So you wanted to shoot me after today." He shrugs, standing to place his empty mug beside me.

He bends and kisses my forehead.

"Go back to sleep."

"Don't go!" I hiss as he turns the door handle. "Please Connor. I don't want to be alone tonight."

His eyes search mine a moment too long. He's going to say no.

"Scoot over."

I place my mug next to his and shuffle over to the wall. Leaving just enough room for Connor. He tucks the covers around me then lies on his back on top of them. I rest my head on his chest and he curls his arm around my back. It takes a few minutes for the tension to leave his muscles.

"It was so real."

He pulls me closer to into his chest. "It was just a dream," he kisses my hair and strokes my back. "or maybe it's your unconscious telling you you've already shot me through the heart," he mutters into my hair.

I can't have moved a muscle since I fell asleep. I raise my head and admire the view. Connor's black eyelashes fan his cheeks. His cheekbones just the right side of sharp. The juicy ripeness of his lips too tempting. I run my fingers over them.

"Oww." Rolling onto my back when Connor nips my finger tips. He rolls onto his side.

"Like what you see?" He smiles slowly, lowering his lips.

We jerk apart when my door slams open. This is beyond a joke.

"There you are Lieutenant," says a most intimidating Lucien.

Connor falls off the bed, quickly pulling himself up to attention.

"Commander."

"I trust you slept well." Lucien's eyes dart to me and Connor's follow.

"Yes sir."

I barely swallow my laugh.

"Good," drawls Lucien, "then you can lead the hunt today."

"Come again?"

"You've been wanting more responsibility. Today's a good day to start, don't you think?"

"But Lucien…"

"That's *Commander* Lucien."

He turns attention to me. "Are you joining us today?"

"Of course." I don't break eye contact.

"Well then…" His grin doesn't fool me. "Happy hunting."

The castle grounds are heaving when I make it outside. Connor is up a tree talking to the crowd. Whilst Lucien leans against a tree directing everyone to Connor.

"There will be three groups. The most experienced will hunt wild boar. The second group will hunt venison and the third will hunt fish. A raven call will sound once when the quota of boar is caught," he lets out a convoluted whistle "twice for the venison," he demonstrates again, "and third for the fishing. Anyone caught hunting after the raven call for their group will be punished. Is that clear?"

He looks each and every member of the crowd. His eyes

soften briefly when they meet mine. Then he's back to dark and dangerous. Rumbles of agreement erupt as folks split into groups.

"Isn't this exciting." Imogen practically squeals as she hooks her arm in mine. "I can't wait for the feast."

"What about the wedding?"

"Oh I'm looking forward to the official part being over, then I can just enjoy Dylan." She grins. "What group are going in?"

"Fishing." Her eyebrows hike. "I'm a vegetarian."

"Since when?"

"Since I killed Thumper and left his forty-three kids starving orphans."

Connor comes over to me and pulls me aside.

"Stay by the river. Don't leave until everyone else does. Whatever you do don't go through the woods until both raven calls have been sounded. OK?"

"Be safe." I stretch up on tiptoes and kiss his cheek.

"Always." He grins. Folks clamber for his attention as soon as he turns away from me.

I end up in a group with older fae and some older children. We make our way through the forest then into the long dewy grass as soon as Brother Michael has finished the prayers for the group. A craggy old pixie takes me under his wing and we meander along the side of the river listening to it gush and gurgle.

He leaves me in a "good spot' with a wooden fishing

pole and some tackle. With last instructions on how to bait and dig out worms from the riverbank he heads further up stream.

I scrabble around in the mud and manage to find a worm. I put it down whilst I try to figure out how to put it on the hook and a bird swoops down and scoops it into its beak. I dig around again. This time I hold the worm between my fingers but the bird dive bombs me and steals the worm just as I drop it.

"Hey, that's stealing," I yell.

The bird lands in a high branch above my head and makes a laughing sound that sounds like "possession is nine tenths, baby."

I give up on worms and ignore the lazy bird looking greedily at me. I put the pole in the water and wait. I make a daisy chain with the few remaining daisies. I look for four-leafed clover but find none. I give up and lie back watching the sun get high through the leaves. Finally my body can't hack the boredom anymore and shuts down.

I jerk as I awaken. I hear a raven call. I listen. Just the one. I get up and wander along the river and then back.

I start walking down edge of the river but soon realize that the only way back to the castle is through the woods. I haven't passed a soul. I must have missed the end of the hunt.

I tentatively enter the woods, looking this way and that but hear nothing. After ten minutes or so I finally begin to relax, fishing pole swinging gently as I walk. I reenact this morning's bed scene, constructing all the things that could have happened if Lucien hadn't been Lucien. I become more and more flushed and more and more flustered. I stop when the feeling that I'm being watched dissolves my fantasies.

A pair of black eyes are peering at me from the low lying bush in front of me. I begin to pant.

"I'm just behind you."

I turn my head to Connor's voice. He's leaning against a tree to my left. Arrow locked and loaded and pointed at the bush. There are two huntsmen behind him, arrows at the ready. I turn my head to the other side and there is Dylan and two Protectors, faces grim.

"Take a slow step back. Keep facing forward," his voice coaxes reassuringly.

I slowly lift my foot and place it behind me. I'm not lifting my next foot until my balance is solid.

"Nice and steady. That's it."

A twig snaps and I freeze. The boar roars and charges. The wind is knocked out of me when my back slams against a tree. Connor grunts and drops from pressing me against the tree to his knees.

"Connor?" He's struggling for breath. "Connor," I shriek as he face plants on the forest floor.

CHAPTER THIRTY-THREE

I drop to my knees beside a crumpled Connor. My violently shaking hands reach out to touch him.

"Connor?" My voice trembles as I gently shake him. Nothing. He's out cold. It's only then I notice the quiver sticking out of his back and the bloodstain surrounding it. Lucien barges the surrounding Protectors out of the way. His face is grim as he takes in the scene.

"Let's get him to the temple," says Lucien, moving to Connor's shoulder. Five Protectors move next to Connor.

"Temple? He needs a hospital."

"Not now Lucy," Lucien's voice is lacking its usual disdain. Gently, on five."

The men heave Connor onto their shoulders Connor grunts despite his unconsciousness as they pace away.

I follow at a close distance. I hear a raven call. Just one. Folks appear through the trees as we pass. The men and women carrying Connor walk at a clipping pace despite their awkward burden.

Sister Sapphire is already waiting on the steps of a sculpted earth building built into the hillside. How she knows to be there, I do not know.

"Take him inside and lay him on the altar. Gently," she says. The Protectors heave Connor up and begin walking. I recognize Connor's work immediately. I am at the heavy wood, glass and metal door, when a thick muscular arm barricades my way. I scowl at the arm and direct my dirtiest look at the owner.

"You can't go in there Lucy," says Lucien. "Sister Sapphire is the best healer in four lands. I'll let you know when there's news."

Joe hurries past Lucien. Lucien tries to stop him as he reaches Connor. They have words. Joe strides on and opens the ornate doors.

I hardly notice when Imogen puts her arm around my waist and leads me to the castle. I've lost my words. She leads me upstairs to the bathing chamber and starts to remove my clothes.

"Let's get you cleaned up shall we," she says softly. I begin to shake when I look at the blood soaked clothes on the floor.

Imogen leads me to the bath and helps me step in. She shoos away the chambermaid and begins to care for me herself. First washing my hair then gently wiping my body with a cloth. I sit shivering in the bath despite the scorching water. She helps me stand up and dries me and wraps me in a towel. She leads me to my bedroom where replacement clothes are waiting, dressing me before towel drying and brushing out my hair.

"Shall we go and keep Joni company?" says Imogen softly.

My catatonic state evaporates instantly. I'm not the only one suffering. Joni is by herself whilst her brother-in-law is fighting for his life. I nod and quickly slip on my shoes as Imogen wraps a cloak around me.

Joni rushes to me as we enter the café and crushes me to her.

"Take a seat," she says leading Imogen and I to a booth.

We slide in opposite each other. Joni quickly places a cocoa in front of me and tea in front of Imogen. I'm unable to drink but my chilled body is glad of the warmth I glean from gripping the mug. The empty café fills with Protectors not able to be in the Temple. All sit silent, praying or talking in solemn whispers. Joni spends the afternoon cooking and feeding everyone.

Day turns to night. Lit tea-lights are placed on all the tables. I get up and pace restlessly towards the window. I have convinced myself that if I see a bright star in the night sky, Connor will be dead.

I am shocked when I look out of the window. The street outside is filled with folks sitting holding vigil. I open the café door and peek out. Between the light from the candles that everyone is holding and the cloud cover, I can't see any stars.

Imogen comes to one side and Joni to the other. They urge me out into the street. We begin walking silently. The

Protectors pour out behind us. Hundreds of us begin walking slowly towards the temple. Imogen, Joni and I sit at the bottom of the steps, the Protectors sit behind us, hundreds of fae fill in behind them.

CHAPTER THIRTY-FOUR

They all begin singing. A slow gentle chant of joy and sorrow. I join in even though I don't know the words. I hum then I mumble what I think they are. We stay like that all night. As dawn breaks, Dylan comes down the steps to us, his face pinched from exhaustion.

"He asked for you few minutes ago."

There must be a tsunami one the other side of the world with the force of our exhaling.

"If you would like, you can see him now," says Lucien who has joined Dylan.

"The rest of you have homes to go to," shouts Lucien as he joins his brother. He reaches and heaves me up onto numb legs. It takes a moment for the blood to begin circulating again so that I can walk.

A naked Connor is lying covered to the waist in a sheet. He's almost the same color as the silver veined white marble slab. Sister Sapphire is sitting at his head, eyes closed with her hands on his forehead. Brother Michael holding prayer beads in one hand is sitting at his feet chanting. An exhausted Joe is sitting with his back against a pillar. I go to him first and lay a hand on his shoulder. He looks up and gives me a tired smile. I move nervously towards the altar.

As I approach, Sister Sapphire removes her hands. I look over my shoulder. Imogen and Dylan are huddled together at the back of the temple. Joni has come in and is sitting with Joe. Protectors are filing in reverently one by one. Everyone is watching. I raise tentative fingers to Connor's brow and sweep his hair away. His eyes flicker open.

"Hi," he says, wetting his lips and swallowing.

"Hi."

His eyes devour my face.

"You don't look so hot."

"You don't look so great yourself," I smile. He smiles back. I swallow the lump in my throat.

"I'm so sorry Connor. If I hadn't gone into the woods…"

"Shhh, later," he slurs and closes his eyes.

"Later," I whisper. "When you're back to your normal handsome self." His lips twitch.

"Mr Hot Fire God."

"Oh God!" He laughs before wincing.

His hand lifts and pulls mine from my face.

"I've got something to tell." I bend my ear close to his lips. When I'm nearly there, he turns his head and whispers a shy kiss across my lips.

"Hmm…I like what you have to say." He smiles at me drowsily, eyes closing.

I straighten, turn and burn hotter when I see everyone grinning at me.

*

Not long after, Connor is put on a stretcher and carried to the forge. I follow behind. Lucien hangs back and in silence walks beside me. My guilt gets heavier with each step.

"I'm sorry," I say.

"Why?" Lucien gives me a confused look.

"For getting Connor hurt." Lucien starts to say something but I cut him off. "You said I would hurt him and I did…"

"Lucy…"

"If I hadn't fallen asleep, if I had just listened…"

"Lucy…"

"and stayed out the forest like Connor had told me to."

"LUCY!" Lucien puts his hand on my arm, stopping me.

"What?" I turn and stare at him.

"This isn't your fault," he says quietly.

"Of course it is…"

"The hunt was finished."

"What?"

"Both raven calls had been called. Someone deliberately drove the boar into the lower woods."

"Why?" *Who?*

He sighs and pinches the bridge of his nose. "Lucy, if Connor hadn't been there you would be the one with the arrow in you right now."

"That would have been better than Connor nearly dying."

"As admirable as your Martyrdom, is I doubt you would have recovered quite as well, if at all."

Connor is asleep when we enter his bedroom. Sister Sapphire sits in a chair at the side of the bed doing whatever it is she does with her hands. When Connor wakes, she administers a pungent dark green liquid. I sit at the other side of the bed feeling useless. Lucien shoos all the milling Protectors back to the barracks. After a few hours he wakes up and drowsily drinks water and asks for more. I take the empty glass downstairs to refill. I stop on the last stair when I hear voices.

"How is he?" asks Dylan.

"Healing nicely," says Lucien.

"Can I go up?"

"Lucy is with him." They look at each other and give identical half grins. How did I not notice they're brothers? They both pick up their mugs to drink at the same time. Lucien stops before he takes a drink.

"I'm sorry," mutters Lucien.

Dylan chokes on his tea.

"You're apologizing? Quick, ring the bell. This is a momentous day in history everyone. We need to record it." He looks around as if addressing a crowd. "Lucien, Commander of the Queens guards is apologizing. FOR THE FIRST TIME EVER!"

"I had meant for you to hear about it before the marriage mart. I was waiting all morning for you to confront me.

Then the podium was set up."

"I'll bet you were sweating."

"Buckets!" The brothers laugh.

"I was watching you the whole time. Waiting for you to make your move. You were sitting there laughing and happy. I thought you were going to get in line or dive up onto the podium and kneel at Imogen's feet. Then I saw you talking to Lucy…the look on your face."

"Would you have gone through with it?" asks Dylan quietly.

"Yes, but I wouldn't have liked it." Dylan's jaw ticks. "Not because of Imogen. I could tolerate a marriage to Imogen, just." Lucien hurries on. "The whole time Garth was talking I had images of you going to the dark place again. Then when you said you'd rather die." A look of utter desolation crosses Lucien's face.

"I'm sorry I said that. I know how much pain it caused you and mum the first time," says a shamefaced Dylan. "I had enough of the priesthood first time round. Besides, I can fulfill my spiritual service better as Imogen's husband."

"Thank god for Lucy," sighs Lucien.

"Admit it, you like her," laughs Dylan.

"Yes, but don't tell her I said so."

I creep as quietly as I can back upstairs.

"It's rude to listen in to other people's conversations."

"Sister Sapphire, you scared me!"

She passes me in stony silence, and I look up to see a pale Connor clutching the doorframe. I run up the last few stairs and put my head under his arm and haul him into bed.

"Don't worry about Sapphire; she's just being an over

protective mother. Besides, she was eavesdropping at the top of the stairs."

"Mother?"

"Yes. She's Lucien and Dylan's mother."

"But she's a Priestess."

"Well, she's more of a healer. She was about to take her vows when she met Lucien and Dylan's dad. She quickly married him and became our healer. Dylan's dad was Commander here before Lucien. He was killed when Dylan was twelve saving a family in a flood. Lucien was only seventeen when he became Commander and became completely overtaken by his responsibilities. Dylan didn't cope very well with essentially losing his dad and his brother. Sister Sapphire left to finally become a priestess and took Dylan with her. He hated the Priesthood. When he came back here his life force was so drained he was barely alive. Imogen was Queen by then and ordered him back into the Protectors."

"First nobody thought to tell me Dylan was Lucien's brother, now this. Nobody tells me anything," I say, huffing as I cross my arms over my chest.

"Don't be mad, Luce. We all know each other's stories here. I forget that this is new information to you." He entwines his fingers in mine. My fingers tingle where he touches. "Still friends?"

When Connor next falls asleep, I dash all over the place getting ingredients for my gran's chicken soup. Seeing Connor half dead has awoken the nurturer in me.

"I swear by the restorative powers of this soup," I smile, sensing his frustration. "So you may be up and about sooner than you think."

Without thought I climb onto the bed and kneel astride Connor's leg. He leans forward and I slowly feed him each mouthful. His hands glide up my thighs to hold my hips. I'm getting edgier with every mouthful. I'm tingling all over. By the last mouthful my hands are shaking.

I place the bowl and spoon on the tray at the side of Connors bed. I wipe his mouth and drop the napkin back on the tray.

"You missed a bit." He points to his lip.

He tilts his lips as I drop mine.

"Not disturbing you, am I?"

Imogen pokes her head round the door. Our heads swerve and my lips graze his ear. Connor's head thumps back against the headboard. I climb off Connor, only when he finally releases his grip.

"I'm here to steal your girl away." The corner of Connor's mouth turns up.

"Oh Imogen, I'm not really up for celebrating tonight."

"Non-sense!"

"Someone needs to stay with Connor."

"I'm fine Luce," says Connor touching my hand. "Go have fun." I search his eyes for a moment.

"If you're sure…" *If I must.*

I pick up the tray and turn back for one last look when I reach the door. His eyes are already closed.

CHAPTER THIRTY-FIVE

Imogen laces her arm through mine and we stroll to a part of the castle I have never been to before. We walk into what is essentially a spa. There are women everywhere waiting to serve. There is a tiled pool with steaming water and fragrant herbs. I smell lavender, rose and geranium. There are three beds laid out in an antechamber. There is a small bath with bubbling brown mud.

Fiona is already there, and unashamedly naked. She has the physique of a warrior princess.

"What is it?" whispers Imogen.

"Fiona frightens me," I say as quietly as I can.

"What are you two whispering about?" she bellows, bending one leg to rest her foot on the bench. Oh God! Nothing is hidden.

"Fiona? She is the biggest-hearted most generous fae I known."

"I'll take your word for it."

Imogen holds her arms out and moves to embrace Fiona. I hug Fiona, trying to keep a gap between our bodies. It's difficult with her enormous breasts.

"Get your kit off then," she roars.

We are pampered to within an inch of our lives. We are pointed to the sauna, then the plunge pools, then the mud bath, then the cold showers. We are given hot stone massages, then a top to toe aromatherapy massage so good I wake myself up snoring. When I wake there's a blue tattoo on my arm. I pull the skin towards me so I can see it better. It's a tattoo of a naked woman with enormous breasts and Grand Canyon hips and a swirling symbol at her belly and a tree growing up from her vagina.

"What is it?" I ask.

"It's the Celtic Goddess of fertility," says Fiona.

"What?" I screech, before accidentally rolling off the bench and landing on the tile floor.

"I can't have this! I'm only sixteen." And Connor and I have enough going on between us. "Oh God, get it off." I lick my fingers and try scrubbing my upper arm. It's not coming off.

"Relax, Lucy," says Imogen. "All the women get the tattoo for the wedding. It's similar henna only it's made of woad. It's to increase the chances of the bride getting pregnant. The more women that carry the energy, the more chance there is of a baby."

"Abstinence until it's gone, darling," snorts Fiona.

"What about kissing?" I say tentatively.

Fiona sits up, astonished. "Didn't your mother tell you can get pregnant from kissing?"

"*What?* No! Oh God, can you?" The rules might be different here. My voice betrays my panic. Imogen and Fiona burst into fits of laughter.

Imogen and I have a glass each of champagne, while Fiona

has several. I sit wide-eyed and incredulous as Fiona gives Imogen advice for her marriage bed from her vast and um... *interesting* experiences. We walk Fiona to her suite. She's glowing. Her Amazonian beauty is growing on me the more I get to know her. Then Imogen and I curl up at the window seat in Imogen's bedroom, curtains closed behind us so we can watch the wedding preparations without anyone knowing.

As we sip elderberry tea several carts filled with flowers arrive. The faerie men tie up the horse and fly down to help the flower maidens riding with them. Several carts laden with meat and vegetables have already passed us to go round to the kitchen. Trolls are hauling huge wooden tabletops under one arm, wooden benches under another. Pixies are rolling wooden kegs through the front doors like logs down a river. They are practically dancing. There are a lot young faerie girls sitting about weaving their flower hairbands for tomorrow, giggling as the males show off to them. There is a cacophony of noise, whistling, singing, shouting, and flirting. We are not getting our beauty sleep anytime soon.

Our dresses for tomorrow are draped over mannequins in the corner. I'm to wear an asymmetrical ankle-length evening gown in an autumnal inky blue silk with a silvery-gold gossamer over-layer. Imogen is wearing a strapless white gown with a heart-shaped neckline. The heavy silk gathers under her bust and drapes to the floor. It is the simplest wedding gown I've ever seen and yet it is the most strikingly beautiful.

"Nervous?" I ask.

"A little. But it wouldn't be a sacred commitment if it was easy to make."

"How did you know Dylan was the one?"

"I wish I could tell you. I just knew. It wasn't love at first sight. We had friendship first. Then love wrapped itself round us and entwined us together. Maybe that was why it was so hard to get together. We were already in love as friends, so it took a little while to recognize that we were in love as lovers too. What about you?"

"I wish I knew," I sigh. "I couldn't keep my eyes off Connor from the first moment I laid eyes on him. How can I be sure that's love and not just lust? I'm sure I'm in love but is it true or will it burn out quickly?" I shrug. "But in a way, it's not the most important thing. Before I came here and did all the work you had me do I would never have dared look at a guy like Connor, never mind have the courage to go on a date or kiss with him. I mean, he's so handsome he's practically divine. He has an incredible body. And he's smart and patient and kind and caring and strong. He should be in a box marked *too good to be true*. But you know what I've realized?" Imogen shakes her head at me. "I'm smart and kind and gentle too. And I'm sweet and I'm funny and I'm beautiful. Really beautiful, because I'm me."

"Maybe we should put Connor and you in that *too good to be true* box together?"

Imogen laughs and we lay our mugs on the floor and climb into bed.

We giggle until we fall asleep.

It's still dark when Imogen wakes me. She's not the excited bride this morning but her indomitable regal self. It's so cold I struggle to get out of bed. I lace up my boots, don my cloak and gloves and hurry after Imogen. She lights two lanterns and hands one to me and we hurry to the clearing.

The day starts with a lit procession to the Emerald Loch. As it's the highest peak in the Flowerlands, it's seen as the place closest to God, ergo easier for the divine to hear the prayers of thanks. Imogen leads, Brother Michael and Sister Sapphire follow. Then it's King Garth, Queen Fiona, Dylan and King Andrew. The Protectors spread out either side of the procession. They space themselves evenly down the line of faeries. They are like fiber-optic cable; they are the outer layer that strengthens the community and allows their energy to flow where it is needed. Without them providing a container the energy would dissipate before it could be used. I didn't get it at first when Connor said they were like Samurai. I see now how the purer their minds, bodies and spirits are the stronger their container, the more they are able to hold and support their community.

I dawdle at the side until Dylan grabs my hand and tucks my arm in his so that I walk beside him. The walk is made in contemplative silence. As we reach the top, the sun is just beginning to peak over the hilltops. The sky quickly becomes slashed with cool purples, pinks and gold.

We all gather in a circle. Brother Michael, Sister Sapphire and Imogen stand in front of us. Brother Michael begins the ceremony, directing us to ponder everything we have sown and everything we have reaped. To give thanks for all the abundance that has been bestowed on us this year.

"We all have a lot to be thankful for. Take time to give

thanks for the flowers that have bloomed. Thanks for the babies that have been born. Thanks for our health. Thanks for the successful harvests of grains in Garth's lands, for our flowers that provide oils and remedies. Thanks for all the food mother earth has provided for us in the forest and beyond. Thanks to the animals that have sacrificed themselves for us. Thanks for our clothing. Thanks for our homes. Thanks for our friends and family. Thanks for our community. Thanks for all the love in our lives.

"Take time to count your blessings for all the good you have received this year. Breath in and fill your heart with gratitude until it is filled to overflowing. In and out. In and out. Fill your whole body with gratitude. Let gratitude flow out of you. Let it overflow out to your neighbor, to your family, to your friends, to all the folks here today, to the hills and mountains, river and lakes, the seven seas, to the animals, the plant kingdoms and the humans. Keep breathing that gratitude out, to the trees and to all the continents and to every being on this planet. And to mother earth herself with deepest gratitude for her allowing us to live on her beautiful planet."

I sit pondering all the things I've taken for granted in my life. Like my mum and dad and our house and hot and cold running water. Food in the fridge, supermarkets, central heating, new clothes, holidays, friends, education, parks. I could go on forever. I see gratitude coming out of my heart floating like faerie dust all over the world until I see it coating everyone and everything. I feel so light I could float away.

"Now, everyone bring your awareness back into your body, back to the here and now," says Brother Michael. I come back slowly. "Before we leave to enjoy a shared brunch, I would like to give special thanks to our brother Connor for his bravery and tenacity in bringing our Lucy to us."

My eyes well when I realize the community have accepted me as one of them now. "Before we go I would like us all to give thanks to Lucy who has shown herself to be one brave young woman. She has come here and done everything we asked of her stoically and without complaint." I duck my head as everyone turns to me and starts murmuring their thanks.

We stand up and people stand about chatting in groups while some crazy fools strip and dive in the freezing cold water, yelling and screaming. Eventually everyone starts heading for home. "Coming?" asks Imogen, extending her arm.

"I'll follow. I'd like to say goodbye. I don't think I'll be back here before Spring."

I sit down on a rock until the last of the stragglers disappear. I kneel at the loch's edge and look at my face. Looking at every little perfect thing about it. "I love you, you are so beautiful." I stand up and look around, making sure I haven't missed anyone. I strip quickly, laying my clothes on a rock. Then go back to the water's edge.

"My toes are beautiful I love my toes. My ankles are beautiful. I love my ankles." I work my way up my legs over my hips and bottom, over my tummy, my ribs, my back, my breasts, my neck and my face. "I love you, I really love you. You are beautiful exactly as you are," I say to my reflection, and grin.

A biting wind has risen and is trying to cut me in two. I

dress as quickly as I can, but my shivering body and chattering teeth make it difficult. I start to jog down the hill in an attempt to heat myself up. I only go a little way before I catch sight of Lucien.

"What are you doing here?"

"Waiting for you."

"You weren't watching me, were you?" I ask suspiciously.

"I came down here to ensure you weren't disturbed."

"Thank you."

"You're most welcome. I came to say thank you for all you've done here. Seeing as it's a day of thanks and all that."

"Thanks, I guess," I say. Something in his demeanor makes me ask the question I've grown afraid of. "I'm not going home, am I?"

"I don't get to decide that."

"Who does? Imogen? I'll speak to her and tell her I want to stay."

"God decides, Lucy."

How do I convince an entity I'm not sure I believe in to let me stay?

CHAPTER THIRTY-SIX

I drag Imogen away from Dylan and we hit the ground running. I'd planned a nice leisurely afternoon. It isn't to be. The palace is full of women. We are scrubbed clean; our hair washed and dried then styled to within an inch of its life.

Flowers have attached themselves to the straps, neckline and bottoms of our dresses overnight. Delicate flowers of pale pink, purple and white. Dark green leaves weave between the flowers, trailing up to the waist round the shoulder.

I dress first. I don't know the seamstress who lifts my dress, careful not to disturb my hair. I haven't seen Tatiana seen since the hunt. My hair is pleated with a few tendrils left loose. Flowers matching my dress twine throughout my hair. Flowers seem to fly to the tips as I slip on matching ballet flats. I look and feel incredible.

It's a far cry from the last time I got dressed up. My sixteenth birthday. I remember looking in the mirror, twisting and turning to check myself out from all angles. I remember sighing, my shoulders sagging. Looking at myself, saying, *the last sixteen years haven't made me pretty; they've just made me fat.*

"What is it?" I say, when mum comes in. "It's the dress isn't it? I look hideous! I'll go change." Mum shakes her head.

"You look amazing," she says, coming to stand behind me and hug me.

"You have to say that. You're my mother. It's in your job description – under lies to tell your kids to make them feel better."

I lean my head back against mum's shoulder taking comfort from the sentiment even if I don't believe the words.

The dressmaker shoos everyone away and dresses Imogen herself. Her Majesty steals my words. I'm not sure if it's dew or jewels that cause the dancing rainbows as she turns round. Her dress makes her natural beauty stand out even more. Her wings seem to have grown overnight and they sparkle like dew in the morning sun. Imogen's jet-black poker straight hair shines past her waist. Her feet are bare. She wants to feel reality when Dylan commits to her. She puts on her crown of pink and purple flowers, mistletoe, ivy and babies-breath has been placed upon her head. This isn't only a wedding. Dylan is to be crowned Prince Consort.

We make our way down to the foyer, where King Garth is waiting. He hands us crystal glasses filled with a pale blue fizzy drink. I sip and sneeze as the bubbles of the lavender champagne go up my nose. I finish it in two delicious gulps. Someone knocks loudly at the door. I wobble slightly as I go to answer it. My jaw drops when I see Dylan. He wears only his dress trousers, feet and torso bare. A mask is painted around his eyes and nose. Blue, green, pink, purple and gold shimmer and blend like an oil spill. The same colors decorate his shoulders.

"Like it?" He wiggles his eyebrows at me and twirls round and flutters his wings suggestively. I giggle and step aside. Lucien clears his throat. I give him the once over as he passes me. He manages to look both menacing and mighty fine with silver and black face and body paint over those highly sculpted muscles. He looks back at me sternly. I sober up instantly. Dylan has zeroed in on Imogen and is standing in front of her, awe-struck, holding her hand. He doesn't take his eyes from her as he speaks.

"King Garth, may I marry Imogen today so that you may have another son and brother in your family, as your family becomes my family?" says Dylan.

"You may."

"Lucien, may I marry Dylan today so that you may have another daughter and sister as part of your family, as your family becomes my family?" says Imogen.

"You may."

Dylan lets out a heavy breath and crooks his arm for Imogen.

A huge cheer goes up as they exit the castle. King's Andrew and Garth walk behind them. Lucien escorts Fiona. I follow.

"May I?" says a voice to my right as I exit the castle. I turn and gasp.

Connor is leaning against an oak pillar, one leg crossed casually over the other, arms folded. Like Dylan and Lucien he is wearing only his dress trousers and his face and body are painted in metallic blues and greens.

I nod at him. He straightens and comes and takes my arm, whispers, "You are beautiful." Not I look beautiful but I am beautiful.

I am grinning, along with the exuberant crowd.

For all the preparation, the poetic ceremony is quickly over. Someone plays a haunting composition on a harp. Someone else gets up and sings a love song. Dylan and Imogen promise love, fidelity and truth in all things. Their hands are bound together with silk cord and they are pronounced man and wife. A huge cheer erupts as Dylan kisses the bride. Imogen smiles serenely at everyone and Dylan grins like the Cheshire cat. Dylan kneels and Imogen crowns him Prince of the Flowerlands. A smaller version of Imogen's crown is placed on his head. They glide through the throng of people congratulating them, wishing them well, and giving them few unrepeatable suggestions for when things go bump in the night.

The wedding party follow Dylan and Imogen to the clearing. Connor leads me to one of the tables that have been set out. He pulls out a stool and motions for me to sit. Connor picks up a brush. Silence crashes over the clearing.

"May I?" Hushed whispers ensue as I nod my head.

Lines of concentration wrinkle Connor's brow as he works away diligently.

"Finished!" He puts down the brush and closes the wooden lid over the make-up. Connor picks up an ornate hand mirror and gives it to me. "Take a look."

My eyes widen in awe at the intricate details of the metallic cobalts, emeralds and golds that now decorate my eyes and nose.

"Amazing job." I beam at him. Other people think so to. They congratulate Connor and slap him on the back as they pass.

I realize when I look at Connor that it matches his mask precisely. I look around noticing only some of the masks match.

"What does a matching mask mean?" I frown as Connor swallows nervously.

"It's a claiming ritual."

"Claiming?"

"Yeah," His face is on fire. "It means you belong to me now."

"WHAT?" Heads turn.

"It also means I belong to you."

"Oh!" *Hmm…* "For how long?" Connor gazes shyly at me through lowered lashes.

"For as long as you want me. Tonight, tomorrow, forever if you like."

We wander through the dusk. A few russet and gold leaves still cling to the mostly bare trees. The wedding celebrations are being held in the banqueting hall of the castle in deference to the changing weather. There is a welcoming fire burning in the huge fireplace. In the corner furthest from the fire stands a six-tiered caked decorated with flowers and gold painted ivy cascading from the top down every tier. Candles burn in wall sconces. Autumn and winter foliage covers everything. Boughs of trees, autumn leaves, holly, and green glossy leafs, apples, pumpkins, unshelled nuts, shimmering glass bobbles twinned together to create table and wall decorations. Heart shaped wooden tea light holders wrapped in mistletoe line the tables. Tall windows are draped in gold voile. Faerie lights are strung across the whole ceiling making it look like a blanket of stars.

Imogen gasps as she enters. She and Dylan twirl around slowly, taking everything in. I stand at the door nervously.

Imogen looks at me.

"You did this?"

I nod shyly.

"It's beautiful, isn't it, Dylan?" But he's already moved off.

Above the fireplace hangs a six-foot portrait of Dylan and Imogen. It turned out well, much to my relief. There were times when I was up an eight-foot ladder that it could have gone either way. Instead of the usual pose of Dylan standing behind Imogen with his hand on her shoulder, both of them looking forwards, regal and untouchable, I decided to paint the raw vulnerability of Dylan's proposal. He's on his knees declaring his love, while Imogen is standing looking down on him, dismayed and delighted. Lucien stands to the right. Fiona, Garth and Andrew to the left. I have painted them in the background but witnesses to this important moment.

"It's amazing, Lucy," gushes Imogen. She turns to me and grabs my hands. "Promise me you won't let your talent go to waste. Promise me."

"OK, I promise." I laugh. Imogen and Dylan move off to welcome their guests.

The place is jumping. There are several hundred faeries in the banquet hall all being fed and watered. It is hot and loud. I am sitting next to Connor enjoying his family and friends. We speak little as I can barely hear him over the joyous babbling of the crowd. With speeches made, toasts drunk and bellies sated, everyone rallies to prepare for the dancing. Only a few tables remain, everything is pushed back to the edges of the hall. Most folks stand. Only the very old and the very young sit. The band strikes up.

The happy couple begins a slow waltz covering the whole dance floor so that everyone gets to see them. Other couples join them on the floor.

"May I have this dance?" He holds a hand out to me. I take it and allow myself to be led to the dance floor.

Connor tugs and I land in his arms. One hand rests on his shoulder, the other on his back and we waltz. I dance properly for the first time in my life. When the song ends, a slower number begins. He puts his arms around my waist. I put mine round his neck. Lucien comes and taps Connor on the shoulder. Connor glances at him and pulls me closer.

"No chance. Make sure that lot over there know it too," he says, jerking his head to the grinning Protectors. He dances us to the center of floor. There we hold on to each other. I put my head on his shoulder and we move around slowly.

In what seems like minutes, the band takes a break. The cake is cut and gallons of tea poured. Connor gets us cake whilst I get tea. Another band is tuning up on stage.

"Ladies and gentlemen, let the fun begin." They start a toe-tapping melody. Couples form a line on the dance floor. I spot Joe and Joni in the middle. Imogen and Dylan at the end.

"Come on." Connor pulls me up until we are standing at the top of the line.

"What's going on?" I shout at Connor.

"Wait and see." He grins cheekily at me. Imogen and Dylan hold hands and start skipping up the line whilst everyone claps and cheers. They stop just past us and start kissing. I look at them and look at Connor. He points. I look up and there is a bush of mistletoe dangling from the ceiling. Dylan comes and stands next to me. I look at Connor and shake my head and try escape. Dylan's arm braces against my back and pushes me back in line. "Lucy, you made me get up and propose to Imogen in front of everyone. Now it's your turn."

We shuffle slowly down the line, not slowly enough for my liking. Couples newly married, long time married, newly together, people in the line for the fun of it. An old wrinkled couple shuffle up the line and kiss under the mistletoe. I hold my heart and 'aww'. Oh no, only five more couples. Fiona and Garth, no make that Fiona and Lucien and Garth and a man I don't recognize. I turn my head and raise an eyebrow to a Dylan grinning.

"It's his long time lover. Garth's been waiting to come out for years. I guess Lucien's proposal forced all our hands."

Finally we are at the bottom of the line and Connor takes my hand to run the gauntlet. I look at him. He smiles encouragingly at me. The crowd is going wild. They are clapping hard and stamping their feet. The noise is deafening. "We don't have to do it if you don't want to."

We walk slowly up the line. I'm so nervous I'm shaking. We get to the end and stand under the mistletoe. Connor steps towards me. He places his hands on my waist and looks deep into my eyes.

"It's only fun, Luce." Not for me.

I shake my head and step back. "Not yet."

The crowd begins to boo. My cheeks burn. Tears coat my lashes, doubling my humiliation. I hug my arms round my waist and hasten away.

Connor finds me nestled on a cushioned window seat at the end of a dim corridor. The window cooling my flaming cheeks.

"I didn't mean to embarrass you," I mutter, my breath fogging the glass. Connor lifts my feet, scoots to the other end of the ledge. Our legs are stretched out, touching.

"I'll live."

"No thanks to me," I mumble.

"I'm fine Lucy."

Minutes pass. I feel Connor's eyes on me as I stare at the diamond encrusted sky.

"It's not that I didn't want to. I did."

"I know." I turn my head.

"Do you?"

"Yeah." His warm gaze loosens something in me. "Come back to the party."

*

The lighting has been dimmed to a romantic glow when we return to the hall. The music has mellowed and faeries have coupled off. Imogen and Dylan stop dancing as I lead Connor onto the dance floor. Dylan hugs me fiercely, Imogen more gently.

"Beautiful girl." Imogen cups my cheek.

I look back as we reach the center. She's watching me with a sadness I can't fathom.

I take Connor's hands and place them on my waist. I wrap my arms around his neck. Laying my cheek against his chest as his cheek lays against the top of my head. As sway close, moving little, one word strikes me –

"Time to go." *Home.*

"Huh?"

"Party's over."

I look around. There is only us on the dance floor. A few fae are sleeping around the edges. There is no music. The band has passed out. I take Connor's hand and lead him to the castle doors. There is the merest hint of light.

"Let's watch the sunrise?" Connor smiles gently at me.

We walk entwined to the river's edge. Connor sits knees bent. I follow, nestling between his legs. My back to his front. Cheek to cheek.

The sky dragon heaves a flaming breath. The sky turns

from indigo to cobalt, violet and sienna. The water turns to molten lava. So beautiful.

"Conn?"

"Yeah?"

"Why did you bring me here?"

"We were asked to help you."

"By whom?"

"Several sources." I feel his shoulders lift and drop. I twist to look at him. "Lucky me, I was assigned the task." He smiles, gently sweeping my hair away and resting his chin on my shoulder.

"Lucky me, you mean."

"Yeah, you definitely got lucky Luce."

"I like it when you call me that."

"What, Luce?"

"My friend Gregor is the only one who still calls me that."

"Was he the one trying to ram his tongue down your throat?"

I gasp. "You were watching?" Something occurs to me. "You were jealous!"

"Was not." His cheeks flush as he stares at the fiery sky.

"You were!" I'm facing him now. "You brought me here before he could kiss me again, didn't you?" I eye him suspiciously. "How long were you watching me?"

"Two years."

"Since Nana died and," I gasp. His blush deepens as his eyes lock with mine. "Since you last had a girlfriend."

"When I first saw you, I knew."

"Knew what?" I frown.

"That you were the one I've been waiting for." I open and close my mouth a few times.

"If you were the one who brought me here, how come it was Dylan sitting with me?"

"I was off getting a tongue lashing from Lucien. And anyway, I didn't want my face to be the first thing you saw in case you hated me for bringing you here."

"No, Conn. I could never hate you. I'm happy to spend my life here."

"With me?" he asks shyly.

"With you."

"Lucy I know we haven't talked about the future…"

"*Shhh.*" I place my fingers over his lips. "We have forever to talk about it, right?"

He covers my hand with his own and places it over his heart.

"Forever," he whispers, eyes glistening.

He leans his a head over a little way and waits for me to tilt my lips towards him. He bends his head a little more until our lips are touching. Tentatively our lip come together in the sweetest gentlest of kisses. Bliss!

Connor lays back taking me with him. Our lips refusing to part now they are finally together. I lay pressed against him without a nanometer separating us.

It's not just the sky that is on fire. My body burns with the need to get closer to Connor. I press myself against him until not even air can fit between us. Until we are completely fused. We lay chest to chest, groin to groin. My whole body tingles, some parts more than others.

More, I need more.

My tongue sweeps his lips until his mouth opens. My tongue slips into Connor's mouth seeking his. Thrust, parry, thrust parry. It's glorious.

I need more. Much more

My hands twine in his hair. One of his hands runs through my now loose hair to cup the base of my skull, the other is pressing across my shoulder blades, compressing my nipples into his chest. It's Heaven.

I groan into his mouth. Our groins press hard against each other.

I need more.

I press my body harder against his. Connor groans, deepening the kiss. Devouring me, devouring him.

I need more.

No, I need air.

We lift our heads to gulp. We stare, breast bones heaving. I tenderly sweep his hair back from his face. He looks up at me with such wonder. My heart becomes so full a single tear glides down my face. Connor touches it reverently with the tip of his finger.

I wrap my hands in his and lay my head on his chest. Our two hearts beat as one.

"It will never be my first kiss but it will be my last first kiss." I slur, suddenly tired. I hope he knows what I really mean.

Just as I'm about to go under Connor whispers,

"I love you."

I'm too drowsy to say it back. I give his hand a little squeeze. It will be the first thing I say when I wake up...

MANY THANKS TO

Claire Wingfield for taking this lump of coal and cutting and polishing it into the sparkler it is today. You took me to my limits and beyond them with a gentle sensitivity that allowed my writing to flourish. Many, many thanks for not only your editorial skills but for your encouragement and belief in E@TP. This book would not be what it is today without you.

Dan Prescott @ Couper Street Type Co. for creating a stunning book cover that enticingly beckons to the magical world inside. I'm in awe of your creative talent. Your way with words ain't too shabby neither!

My beautiful friends: Adelle, Fotoula and Trisha. Thank you for coming along for the ride. I'm flying high on a carpet weaved with your belief, support and love.

My children who bore the brunt of my artistic temperament, essentially I wanted to write and they wanted to be fed! I love you to the end of the last universe and back … and then some.

NOTE TO READER

There's more! I'm not finished with Connor and Lucy. To be more precise they're not finished with me.

If you'd like to find out if Lucy and Connor survive being in two different worlds or indeed you would like find out more about what I'm up to or would like more inspiration you can find me at the following world wide abodes:

www.facebook.com/julie.damour.7

twitter.com/thejuliedamour

uk.pinterest.com/limitlesslifeuk/elephant-the-party/

or you can do it the old fashioned way:
julie@juliedamour.com

Please help other readers find the book by reviewing on Amazon and Goodreads. Your opinion matters!

Can't wait hear what you loved best about the book. Who are your favorite characters? What's your favorite quote?

ABOUT

Julie was born to a land swathed in myth and legend. A magical land where humans and fae still fall in love, faerie kings and queens still care for all of Earth's elements, where fae guardians still protect us and faerie stories are a living breathing part of everyday life.

Julie draws upon her Scottish heritage and her spirituality to create empowering, mystical stories of self-love and acceptance with a generous dash of red hot romance.

When not *'away with the faeries'*, reading, feeding her intellectual curiosity or nurturing her imagination, you will find Julie walking between worlds or the *dear green place* that is Glasgow, where she enjoys interacting with beings of light.

Made in the USA
Charleston, SC
13 November 2016